VERUSKA

I dedicate this book to Vera and Herb Moss for their support and help with this project.

Love you.

Raffy – Los Angeles, CA

I

Prague, Czechoslovakia

Vera opened her eyes, and saw Harold's emerald-green eyes staring at her.

"I love you so much!" Harold whispered.

He was dressed in a white tunic, black pleated pants, and a raincoat.

His hands were running through Vera's blonde hair.

They were holding and staring at each other beneath the stone arches of the central train station in Prague.

It was a very cold day and the sky was gray.

"Listen to your heart before he says good-bye for-ever...Go with the feeling you have inside of your heart." Babushka, her grandmother, gave Vera that advice before she went to the train station.

It had been ten days since Harold and Vera met in Karlovy Vary, Czechoslovakia.

Martin, Harold's father, was in the Brazilian Diplomatic Corps and was transferred to Prague after Edvard Beneš reassumed his position as President. Beneš had gone into exile, in London, after Great Britain and France signed the Munich Agreement which allowed the immediate Nazi annexation and military occupation of Czechoslovakia.

Prior to being transferred to Prague, Martin and his

family had lived in numerous places such as Buenos Aires, Budapest, Rio de Janeiro, Montreal, Vienna, London, Salvador, Montevideo and the Dominican Republic. Now he was the Brazilian Ambassador to Czechoslovakia.

When Great Britain and France failed to keep their promise of defending Czechoslovakia from the Nazi occupancy, Edvard Beneš lost faith in the West. He created an alliance with Russia that allowed the formation of a socialist party into the Czech political system. He was going to preside over a coalition government involving Democrats and Communists. Klement Gottwald would serve as the Prime Minister of the Communist Party and Jan Masaryk would remain as the Foreign Minister.

Martin had a great knowledge and understanding of foreign affairs.

In the wake of all those changes and the increase of the Cold War, Martin believed it was only a matter of time before both parties would clash. So after Martin and his wife returned from their meeting with President Juan Perón and his new wife Eva he decided to relocate the family and the household staff to Rome.

Harold found himself before Vera, carefully studying her face, trying to remember every inch of it.

She was so exquisitely beautiful with her long eyelashes, her eyebrows plucked into perfect arches, full lips, and high Slovakian cheekbones. Her blonde hair was pulled back in a tight bun.

She was wearing a fox coat over long pants.

"I wish I didn't have to move to Rome. I promise you, we will see each other again."

Vera had been watching him for a long time as they stood there.

The last ten days had been so marvelous; she had experienced every emotion: happiness, passion, sexual desire and satisfaction, and now heartbreak and sadness.

Harold pulled her toward him as her head lay against his shoulder. Her silky blonde hair smelled like strawberries against his face.

Suddenly tears appeared in her eyes. She started crying helplessly as he held her in a tight embrace.

He was also hurting inside. He lifted her chin, kissed her lips, and tried smiling.

"I'm sorry! I had promised myself I wasn't going to cry," Vera whispered as she struggled to stop crying.

His strong arms held her in a long and tight embrace as he gave her passionate sweet kisses.

Harold looked into her innocent eyes and kissed her again, hoping time would hold still. Vera was looking at him and hoping for the same thing.

Their hope came crashing down when the sound of the train whistle brought then back to reality. The wheels began to grind.

Harold gave a final desperate tight hug and parting kiss as he looked at Vera for one last moment before boarding the train. He had tears in his eyes.

She waved good-bye at him, wondering when and if they would see each other again.

"I love you, my darling! I will wait for you!" Vera mumbled, feeling helpless.

Vera tried to smile at him.

"You do not know how much those words mean to me," Harold yelled.

The train started to move slowly as Harold yelled again, "I love you!"

Vera's vision was blurred by the tears. She was in love for the first time in her life.

The train started to go faster and faster.

Vera watched the train disappeared over the horizon while she stood at the end of the station platform.

She stood in the rain getting absolutely drenched and she was crying. She couldn't move; tears were consuming her.

"I cannot live without him," she kept telling herself over and over.

Suddenly a loud voice startled her.

"What?" Vera mumbled, confused. "*Where am I?*"

"Veruska, get up! Dinner is ready," her mother was calling from the second floor.

At that moment, Vera realized she was awakened from a dream. She had dreamed about the last time she saw Harold.

Veruska was what her family and her friends called her, especially when her mother was present. They shared the same name, Vera.

Vera lay very still for a few moments, smiling as images of Harold sped through her head. The palace ballroom where they first kissed, the surprise picnic in the woods, their intense daily talks, the feeling of happiness when they were laughing having an Irish coffee at the Brno Caffe. She still could feel the way his lips felt when he was kissing her.

She forced herself to stop thinking about him; otherwise, she would start crying again.

Suddenly, the knock at the door startled Vera from her thoughts.

I drifted off again, she thought.

"Veruska, come, dinner is ready!" Her mother's voice tore her away from her thoughts.

"I'm coming," Vera responded.

She had a smile on her face, as images from her dream were still so vivid in her mind.

II

Vera got out of bed, and walked out of her room.

Vera's room was at the end of the hall overlooking the exquisite garden and ponds in her parents' backyard.

The house was a large three-story rectangular building with glass block and gray stone facing. It was the biggest house in the neighborhood.

She walked down the hall, past her bathroom with imported mosaic title that separated her room from her parents' master suite.

She took the stairs down to the second floor, walking into the living room.

In the middle of the living room, facing the grand stone fireplace and a grandfather clock, were two upholstered chairs and a nice leather sofa. She continued walking into the dinning room where Vladimir, Vera's father, was sitting at the head of the table, reading the newspaper.

"Good evening, Father," Vera said as she kissed his forehead.

"Good evening, Veruska," he replied.

On the center of the dining room table was a flawless Meissen vase.

The individually hand-painted vase was positioned just the right way so the crossed blue swords would be easily seen by anyone looking in that direction. The crossed blue swords on a white background represent the swords of the Saxonian arms and are Meissen's trademark.

Behind Vladimir was a cabinet displaying other Meissen and Rosenthal figurines and vases.

Vera's mother proudly displayed her collection of expensive pieces that symbolized luxurious European porcelain savoir vivre.

Vera walked toward the kitchen where her mother was busy cooking.

"Veruska, please go to the first floor and get your grandmother, Babushka."

"I will," Vera replied as she walked through the carved oak doors leading into the mahogany library.

Floor-to-ceiling hand-built bookcases covered two of the library walls. Colossal paintings covered the other walls. Famous Czechoslovakian artists painted some of the exquisite pieces, and they belonged in a museum.

Vladimir believed in investing in three things: art, diamonds, and gold. He believed they were war-proof investments.

Vera made her way through the library and took the staircase to the first floor, central hall.

Babushka, Vera's grandmother, was near her

bedroom door waiting for Vera.

"Babushka, we are all in the dining room." As she hugged her, she noticed that Babushka had a melancholy expression in her face.

"What's wrong, Babushka?"

"I was remembering your grandfather, how much I loved him." She smiled. He had passed away two months earlier.

"Love? I don't know anything about it." Vera remarked.

"Oh yes, but just remember to take action when the time is right and treasure what life shows you...but don't ever stand in the way of true love. Without our love we would never have made it through your mother's birth, never have bought our first horse or opened our transportation company." She said, as they started to walk upstairs.

"Love is everything. It is the most stable, reliable, and trustworthy feeling in the universe. Veruska, wait until you fall in love." She smiled.

"We will see, Babushka. I'm not sure this will be that important in my life."

"How about that young, handsome Brazilian man that came to the house to pick you up?"

Hiding her true feeling, Vera said, "Babushka, he is gone...who knows if I will ever see him again."

Babushka smiled. "Humm. Love will find you. When you get to be my age there is only one thing that is important, to me, that is."

"And what is that?" Vera asked.

"A small glass of good vodka every night is the most important thing to me."

Both of them laughed.

III

Vera was born in the small northern Czechoslovakian town of Vysoke nad Jizerou the Krokonose Mountains of Bohemia.

Vladimir, her father, was born in Hladove and raised in Znojmo, both in Moravia. At a very young age, he was appointed head of the hospital in Vysoke, which served a wide mountainous area.

He was considered a highly cultured man who was more involved in the welfare of others than of his own family. Perhaps that was why the community held him in highest esteem.

Vladimir was always calm, he rarely displayed his feeling and he always had everything under control, above all he had full control over the entire family.

Vera had begun school in Vysoke when she was eight years old and she remembered, to the surprise of her mother and herself, when Vladimir announced his decision.

"This afternoon, I have resigned as head of the hospital in Vysoke. I decided to do this because it is only a matter of time before Hitler will invade Czechoslovakia and start another war." He paused. "And it is time for Veruska to attend a better school and meet different people, so this is the right time for us to move. In two weeks we are moving to Kladno."

"But, dear..." her mother started to say.

Vladimir raised his hand to stop her from protesting. "Hold on! I haven't finished yet!" he snapped, in a louder voice as he looked at his wife. She lowered her eyes and said no more.

Vladimir married Vera's mother when she was only eighteen, and she totally depended upon him. He made all the decisions.

Vera's mother become accustomed to the habits of strict obedience, she knew better never to argue with him.

"We are moving into your grandparents' house. This way we can help Babushka manage the family transportation business."

He turned to his wife and gave her another of his stares so that she would not interrupt him.

"I'm accepting a position as head surgeon in the General Hospital in Kladno." He stopped for a second, "I'm also planning on opening my own medical practice at our house. The building is large enough to accommodate everything. My office will be on the first floor right next to our family business."

Vera's grandfather had started his own business by buying one horse and wagon and, with that, he began a transportation and moving company.

The timing was perfect, as Czechoslovakia had

become one of the world's ten most industrialized countries when it inherited 70–80 percent of all the industry of the Austro-Hungarian Empire.

Kladno became the historical birthplace of Bohemian heavy industry, becoming the largest city of the Central Bohemian Region.

The small transportation and moving company grew into a very significant Kladno business, first with a fleet of horses and wagons, then with a fleet of trucks.

The year her father decided to move the family to Kladno was the year that the war started, followed by the German occupation of Czechoslovakia.

Prague became the "Fourth City of the Third Reich."

Vera remembered seeing German troops entering Prague when she was nine years old.

"This is the day that Czechoslovakia ceased to exist," Vladimir said.

The country was broken up into districts.

Traces of the Nazis were everywhere.

The Czech monuments were taken down.

Streets and plazas were renamed with Nazis names.

The singing of Czech songs was forbidden.

Vladimir, who had opened his own medical practice in their house and was busy as the head surgeon at the General

Hospital, was also able to shelter his family from the Germany atrocities suffered by the rest of the people.

Some of his patients paid him in currency, others paid with food they had produced: chickens, ducks, potatoes, vegetables.

His family was able to eat quite well though there was a constant food shortage.

It was a period of hunger, fear, concentration camps, death, and above all, no freedom.

Veruska was too young to understand what was happening to her country.

She remembered seeing Germany army vehicles everywhere.

Little by little, everything was taken away from the Jews.

First, the Germans made it mandatory that every Jew had to wear the yellow star.

Then the Jews were not allowed to walk down the street after six o'clock in the evening.

After that, Jews were not allowed to go to restaurants and cafes or to travel.

Ownership by Jews of valuables such as jewelry and gold was prohibited. German soldiers wearing their steel helmets went into every Jewish home and confiscated anything of value.

After that, Jews were to be transported by train to a secret place.

Jews were stripped of their names. A simple numbered tattoo on their arm, such as A-2277, became their name.

One by one, the Jews disappeared, were separated, and eventually executed.

Over seventy thousand Czech Jews died in concentration camps.

Vladimir was able to protect his family from the Gestapo. They left the family alone except for one day when they commandeered Vladimir's 1937 Packard convertible for a high-ranking German officer.

One day during the German occupancy, Vera experienced a harsh taste of Nazi atrocities. One of her best friends while growing up in Kladno, Marek, and his family had to go underground.

It was late afternoon and Vera's two best friends, Eva and Marek, came home with her after school.

Normally Marek would stay until his parents, Alexander and Helena, would stop by and pick him up, occasionally staying for dinner.

His parents worked in Kladno but lived in Lidice, a nearby village.

This day they were invited to stay for dinner.

"Would you like me to set the table?" Eva asked

Vera's mother.

"If you be so kind, Veruska will help you." Vera's mother replied as she and Helena peeled potatoes at the kitchen sink.

"Please hurry up!" Babushka called from the living room. "Vladimir won't give me any vodka until we start eating."

Vladimir and Alexander were seated at the dining room table.

Vladimir was holding up the newspaper, *Pravda*.

"Can you believe all this news about the shooting of the Blond Beast?"

The Blond Beast was the nickname given to Reinhard Heydrich because of his belief in the supremacy of the blond-haired, blue-eyed Germanic people.

"Listen to this!" Vladimir said as he read part of the article out loud:

Reinhard Heydrich, Hitler's right man in Czechoslovakia, was shot seven days ago, while being driven from his country villa to his office in Prague.

When his driver reached the Holešovice section of Prague, two Czech resistance fighters opened fire on his open green Mercedes.

The two gunmen had supposedly been trained in Britain, and had parachuted into Czechoslovakia, as part of what is called Operation Anthropoid.

"Heydrich had become a very arrogant man who believed he could travel without an armed escort, thus showing his confidence in his intimidation of the Czech resistance and his control of the population," Alexander replied.

"Dinner is ready." Vera's mother interrupted.

Vladimir said, "We need to make a toast to Edvard Beneš, the person responsible for *Operation Anthropoid.*"

"Good, now I can have my vodka," said Babushka.

As they were ready to eat, the phone rang. It was an urgent phone call for Vladimir.

"Probably the hospital," Vera's mother whispered.

As Vladimir listened on the phone, he became very pale and worried.

"Are you sure about this? Everyone? That cannot be true!"

Quietly he put down the receiver. He turned slowly and looked at Alexander and Helena.

"What is the matter, dear?" asked Vera's mother.

"Well something horrible and terribly disturbing has happened," Vladimir said, as he continued staring at Alexander and Helena.

"Heydrich died in Bulovka Hospital in Prague from blood poisoning brought on by fragments of auto upholstery, steel, and his own uniform, which had lodged in his spleen."

Alexander looked at him, "Vladimir, you are such a joker. That is certainly good news—we must celebrate one less Nazi pig in our country."

"Yes considering that we were convinced that the assassination attempt had failed as both assassins were not able to kill him...when the first assassin stepped in front of Heydrich's car, trying to shoot him, his.sten gun jammed." Helena said.

"After Heydrich's ordered his driver, SS-Oberscharführer Klein, to stop the car, he made the fatal mistake when he stood up to shoot the first assassin, because that gave enough time to the second assassin to throw the modified grenade at the car. Ironically, the grenade missed the car and end up hitting the pavement and exploding. When the grenade exploded, fragments ripped through the car's right-rear fender, embedding some of the horsehair used in the upholstery into Heydrich's body, causing the fatal blood infection. If Heydrich, the *Butcher of Prague,* had not ordered the driver to stop the car he would still be alive." Babushka said as she grabbed the empty glass in front of her.

"I wish that was it." Vladimir's face hardened.

"Adolf Hitler is totally enraged and has ordered to the Nazi police to hunt down and murder the responsible Czech resistance members and anyone else suspected of being involved in Heydrich's death."

"The Führer is also demanding a highly elaborate funeral for 'the man with the iron heart' and," Vladimir paused and looked directly at Alexander and Helena before continuing, "according to my source, the German security police have surrounded Lidice, your village."

"What?" Alexander screamed, glancing at his wife and grabbing her hand.

"No! This cannot be happening." Helena cried, falling back on the dining room chair.

"Good heavens! Can it be possible?" Vera's mother asked. "I don't believe it." Her tone showed doubt.

An awkward silence fell between them.

"The Nazis chose Lidice because of its residents' known hostility to the occupation and because Lidice was suspected of harboring local resistance partisans," Vladimir continued.

"According to some witness, they claimed that the Nazis blocked all avenues of escape and surrounded the entire population with nowhere to escape."

"Those bastards! We must go home and make sure everything is all right. My brother and my mother were at the house," Alexander said, rising abruptly and heading toward the front door.

"This cannot be true."

"Wait!" Vladimir quickly rushed in front of him and

barred his way. "Hold on, Alexander!"

"This is crazy," Alexander screamed.

"Listen to me! Please..." Vladimir was staring into Alexander's eyes.

"If this is true, do you think you can save anyone?"

"They will arrest you and your family and you will end up like all the others." Vladimir took a deep breath.

"Remember when we had the mass protests years ago and that young medical student, Jan Opletal, was fatally wounded?"

"The Germans retaliated ruthlessly, sentencing nine students to death, closing the Czech universities, and sending twelve hundred students to concentration and labor camps."

They all looked at each other in silence, each contemplating the other's thoughts.

"You have your son, Marek, and your pregnant wife to think about."

"Go on, Vladimir; tell us all you heard," Helena said.

Alexander was silent.

"All males over fifteen years of age have been put in a barn and shot."

"My...My brother!" Alexander's eyes dropped slowly toward the floor.

There was anger and pain in Vladimir's face as he

said, "Sorry, Alexander, all the men in the village are dead. I wish I was wrong but it is true. Another nineteen men, returning from work in a mine, along with seven women, have been sent to Prague, where they have also been shot. The village women are being sent to the Ravensbrück concentration camp, where they will probably die in the gas chambers or from overwork. The children were separated from their parents and are being sent to a Gneisenaustreet a concentration camp in Poland or, if suitable for 'Aryanization,' they are being shipped to Germany."

"Aryanization?" Vera's mother repeated.

"Yes, that was established by the Reich. 'Aryan' means the master or superior race. This superior race was originated in ancient Germany and Scandinavia. The children who fit this description are being sent to Germany for indoctrination."

Vladimir continued, "As you can see, there is nothing you can do right now. We should get more information before we figure out what to do. I will call some people and see if I can learn more. It is far too dangerous and impossible for us to go to Lidice. All the roads leading there are blocked by the Nazis."

Alexander and Helena sat silent and motionless, realizing that they had lost everything: their homes, their youth, their hope, their family.

After a few seconds, Helena got up, put her arms

around Alexander, and said, "Vladimir is right. We cannot go home! We cannot do anything right now. We need to think about Marek and our new addition."

"God help us," Babushka said as she poured more vodka into her glass.

After a restless night, they awakened and the sun was shining.

Helena and Alexander came into the dining room where Vera and Vladimir were drinking some coffee and listening to the radio.

"Please sit down and listen to the news on the radio. Veruska and Marek are outside playing in the backyard."

The Prague radio stations were broadcasting the extermination of Lidice, how all two thousand residents were being punished.

"This is such a crime! They are barbarians! Hitler wants to make sure the entire world learns about the consequences and punishment of any assassination attempt made against the Führer or any high-ranking officer of the Third Reich," Vladimir said angrily.

"The entire village is being bulldozed, all buildings razed to the ground and salt is being poured on the ground so that nothing will grow."

They were all silent, mortified by what was happening in their country.

"I suggest that you go at once to Contessa Ondracek's

country house," Vladimir said. "Given the present situation, it is far too dangerous for you to remain here in Kladno. I already phoned her and arranged for you to go there. Her house is one of the sanctuaries and no one should bother you there. You have to go into hiding until Hitler has satisfied his revenge."

"You are right. We must leave here at once." Alexander raised his eyes and looked at his wife.

Helena turned to Vladimir and said very sincerely, "I shall never be able to thank you enough for all you have done for us."

All of a sudden Helena's face turned pale when she realized that Veruska and Marek were standing next to them listening to their conversation.

She turned around and ran towards the bathroom as she started to feel very sick.

"I promise you, we will see each other again." Marek told Veruska as he hugged her.

Two weeks after the Lidice horror, another Czech village, Ležaky, was also destroyed, the men and women shot, the children sent to concentration camps.

The estimated death toll to avenge the death of Heydrich reached thirteen hundred.

IV

As Vladimir sheltered his family from the Germany atrocities suffered by the rest of the country, he also took total control of everyone's life and destiny, especially of his little girl, Veruska, his only child.

Vladimir was a very strict husband and father, a dictatorial disciplinarian who exercised total control over his wife and Vera.

With the end of the war and the Nazi occupation, Vladimir had decided that Vera should broaden her education while experiencing strict discipline.

He withdrew Vera from the local public school and entered her in a Roman Catholic convent run by newly arrived English sisters.

When Vladimir decided something, that was it, there was no arguing about it because his decision was always the final decision.

Once she started attending the convent, Vera was allowed periodic visits home; otherwise, all her activities were confined to within the four walls of the convent.

When she would visit home, her activities were very sheltered and controlled by Vladimir. Her curfew was set at

8:00 p.m. and her activities out of the house were limited to daytime. Vera was allowed to go only on afternoon walks in the nearby woods or occasionally attend a carefully selected afternoon movie. Otherwise, she could go out shopping with her mother and Babushka or stay home. None of the other kids had such a restrictive father.

This very controlled environment only increased Vera's emotional turbulence.

The feeling of sadness and isolation kept growing inside of her. She would weep at night, as she couldn't help feeling that she didn't belong anywhere. She was having trouble concentrating during classes. Vera felt totally isolated with no friends.

She never earned a word of praise from her father. She felt she had done everything she could to please her father.

She feared her future. She felt lost. She felt terrified.

One afternoon Vera walked into the church and stood right at the entrance, allowing her eyes to adjust to the darkness.

Vera closed her eyes as she recalled what Mother Superior Letsprey had told her the day before: "You will be expected to do God's work in our community and to follow the Catholic doctrine every day rigorously. To teach Catholic values and to preach the Word of God to its members and help the misguided souls so they can better their way by finding God."

She took a deep breath before continuing. "There are no days off when it comes to spreading the word of our Lord. Praying will be your anchor. You will be expected to cleanse yourself of all your sins and you will take a vow of chastity before entering the House of God. Your soul has to be pure and you must fight carnal sin. We will not tolerate any scandal in our abbey."

The church was silent as a tomb, very dark and cold. The stale air was cold and smelled of rotting dead corpses mixed with a musty old smell.

She walked down the aisle, turning right and kneeling in front of the massive marble baroque sculpture of Our Lady in a Halo.

"Please, God, I ask for your help and for you to guide my soul. If only Marek would still be here I would not feel so alone. He would take care of me."

She clasped her hands together and started praying. She prayed for guidance.

Vera was feeling so lost; her life had no purpose. There was a lonely and empty feeling inside of her. She felt very vulnerable. She also found one of her options to escape from her very controlled life would be serving the House of God.

A few hours later, Vera came out of the church looking

very tranquil. There was a great sense of peace that had come over her.

That was the moment Vera had made her decision about her future.

V

"I decided to serve the house of God. I'm becoming a nun," Vera announced to her parents during one of her visits back home. She trembled, and looked at her father anxiously, hoping to get his approval.

Vladimir was stunned for a moment. He stepped away from Vera, walked over to the window, and looked out at the street. He did not know what to say.

After a few seconds, he turned around and raised his eyebrows at her and said, "Bloody Hell!"

"Father!"

"What?…Oh, I'm sorry."

Vladimir felt the blood rushing to his face.

"Surely this is an admirable quest, but this is not what I had in mind when I sent you to the convent." He was struggling to gain control of the situation.

He tried looking calm.

"I hope you recognize the sacrifice you are going to make. Are you sure this is what you want?"

"Yes! This is what I want," she snapped suddenly. "Will you stop it? You…you don't understand. Why can't I do anything right? I've done anything wrong."

Vera started to walk away.

"Wait just a minute," Vladimir replied.

Vera's mother was looking at the concern in Vladimir's eyes. "Vladimir, let her go for now. All of us need some time to think about this. Don't be upset, Vladimir."

Vera ran upstairs to her room.

"This is madness," Vladimir said out loud.

"Why in the name of God does she think she wants to become a nun?"

"Vladimir, please allow me to reason with her in the next few weeks," Babushka pleaded with him.

"Our Veruska is lonely and very vulnerable right now. I believe this is a transitional time for her. We need to be patient. Your little daughter is transforming herself into a woman."

"All right, reason with her. You are probably right. She is confused. We cannot take this religious nonsense seriously. And if this fails, I'm taking matters in my own hands," Vladimir said under his breath.

As the weeks went by, Vladimir realized that Vera wasn't going to change her mind that easily.

When they asked her why she had cut her hair so short she replied, "Why should I bother growing my hair? It is going to be covered up with the habit."

The next day Vera told them she had bought a crucifix to symbolize her faith in God.

"What are we going to do?" Vera's mother asked Vladimir.

Although Vladimir was a practicing Roman Catholic, he was not about to let his only daughter adopt such a life. Vladimir decided it was time for him to take matters into his own hands as usual.

During the following visit home, Vera was sitting in the living room when her father walked by and said, "Veruska, I would like to see you in the library." He was pointing to the doors leading to the library.

Vera followed him passively, closing the door behind her as they entered the library.

She saw her mother quietly sitting on the sofa waiting for her father to start talking.

Vera sensed something was up. Things were going to change.

"Veruska, please sit down," Vladimir instructed.

Vera sat on the sofa, next to her mother.

Babushka sat on the chair next to the sofa drinking her glass of vodka, smiling. She was happy.

"Now, Veruska," said her father, taking a chair, and drawing it in front of the sofa on which she was seated.

"You know your mother and I want the best for you."

Vera glanced at her mother.

"I also want the best for you and I love you, Veruska."

Babushka smiled before taking a sip of her vodka.

"I've come to a decision that you must see more of this word, you need to broaden your cultural background. It would be a good experience for you to broaden your education away from the convent." Vladimir smiled gently.

"A very fine private girls' boarding school would be a good idea."

"But, Father!" Vera was unable to keep quiet.

But Vladimir was not ready to be interrupted.

"No, don't interrupt me, my daughter, let me finish."

Vera nodded as her eyes rested on Babushka.

"Perhaps a boarding school in England, actually one of the best English schools for girls. The name of the school is Saint Mary's Boarding School and it is located in St. Albans."

"You...you want me to go to school in England? By myself?"

"Yes!"

"For how long?"

"One year," Vladimir replied.

"One year!" Vera was stunned that her father was letting her going away for that long. She was also wondering why did wanted her to go so far away.

Vladimir knew the only way she would give up the idea of becoming a nun was to become more independent and to broaden her education.

"The school was founded in 1893 and was built in one of the prime   locations in St. Albans. You will learn a wide variety of subjects. Their program is designed to encourage spiritual growth, leadership, and responsibility with absolute integrity, humility, and perfect manners." Vladimir paused for a second. "You will like the school. The chapel and the majority of the buildings are of Gothic style. There are beautiful gardens with green fields, trees, streams, and ponds. Oh, they also have a stable so on weekends you will be able to indulge in your passions for riding horses and fox hunting."

"Father, can I go to my room and think about all this?"

"Yes, of course, but I already have decided that this is the best thing for you."

Babushka poured herself another glass of vodka and told Vladimir, "Let me go and talk to her. I'm sure England will be very good for her. After all, she is a young woman finding her way into adulthood."

She entered Vera's room and sat right next to her granddaughter. She touched her hand. "Veruska, listen to me."

Vera started pouring out her feeling and fears. "Babushka, why is   everything is always so complicated? Everything I do is always wrong. I can never get Father to tell me I did something right; he is always telling me what I did wrong." Vera embraced Babushka as she had the high-est sentiments of   esteem, respect, and admiration for her.

"My little Veruska, I know how you feel but let me tell you something. Your father loves you very much and he is very proud of you."

"So why doesn't he ever tell me that?"

"Well, there are certain people that are incapable of doing that. He is probably afraid of losing control. He is one of those people that thinks that if he gets too close to you he will not be able to control you. You know what I mean, darling?"

Vera was unable to say anything for a moment.

"I want to make sure you make the right decision. I don't want you to make a decision based on this emotion of isolation. I don't want to wake up twenty years from now thinking, I should have...what if I had...or I could have. If I could be you, I would go to England and enjoy your freedom. If you still have the same urges when you come back then you should continue with your plans."

Babushka sighed.

"Veruska, we just want you to make the right decision." She paused before saying, "Oh, one more thing. I don't care what Mother Letsprey told you, I'm telling you that praying will not satisfy your curiosity and certainly will not stop any carnal desire you might have."

"Babushka! I love you," Vera said as she hugged her.

It took Vera a few days to get accustomed to her new surroundings in England. She missed her friend Eva, her parents, and Babushka.

The year she was in England went by quickly.

She blossomed into a very beautiful and independent young woman.

One afternoon, when she was walking down the street in St. Albans, she saw a gypsy fortune-telling house and on impulse decided to have her fortune told.

A minute later, she was seated opposite Olga, a big fat Gypsy woman with two missing front teeth and a dirty shawl over her head.

As the old Gypsy shuffled the tarot cards Vera was asked herself *What am I doing here? I must be crazy*.

The Gypsy turned up the first tarot card. It was a card of a naked woman with a sheet covering her lower body and she was holding some flowers. "This card is telling us that you have the talents to succeed in life. You simply need to finish what you've started to reap the benefits."

The Gypsy turned a second card it was a chariot being pulled by two horses that appeared to be going in separate directions.

"Ahhh, this card represents a very dramatic change will be happening in your life but before this dramatic change will take place you will be going through many conflicts; however, everything is going to be all right in the end. Just go with your instincts."

The next tarot card was of two lovers holding each other, and a third person was behind them with her arms open to the sky.

"Ohhh, this is the lovers' card." She smiled. "It points to new love, attraction, and sex but it isn't always as it seems. It can indicate a failed relationship, unfaithfulness, and separation as well."

"This card that you picked is the high priestess card. She represents your intuition. She's the guardian of secrets, which can be a positive or negative thing, depending on whether you want to know, keep, share, or avoid disclosing. Trust your instincts; they're always right, but watch out for emotional insecurity. You almost made a wrong decision because of your insecurity."

Vera rose to her feet. "Oh look at the time. I need to go back to school. Thank you." Vera smiled before running out of the room.

Everything will be fine now, she told herself.

A year had passed. Vladimir, Vera's mother, Babushka, and Vera's friend Eva were at the Ruzyne airport waiting for the flight from London to arrive.

"I see her—she just got out of the plane." Eva was pointing to the plane.

'Where?" Vera's mother asked anxiously.

"She is wearing a velvet blazer and knee-length pencil skirt, high heels, and sunglasses," Eva said as she started to wave to Vera. "Her hair is long, down past her shoulders."

Vera's pencil skirt was accentuating all her curves and she looked flawless.

"That's not Veruska!" her mother insisted.

"Eva is right! That young woman is our Veruska," said Babushka.

Our Veruska has come of age, Babushka thought to herself.

All of a sudden, Vera started waving back. She felt nervous and a bit lightheaded seeing her family after such a long time.

When Vladimir spotted Vera, he realized that his little girl had become a beautiful and gracious young woman.

He also realized that soon she was going to be an object of love and   admiration to many men.

One thing Vladimir could not see was that she had become an independent and liberated young woman.

VI

A few months after Vera returned to Czechoslovakia, her parents decided to take Vera to Karlovy Vary for a long weekend.

For Vladimir it was a way of celebrating the fact that Vera had no intentions of going back to the convent.

Eva, Vera's best friend, also came along. Like Vera, Eva was an only child and the same age. Their parents were best friends. They had gone the same school and taken the same classes. They lived four blocks apart. They considered each other the sister each had never had.

They shared everything with each other, so when Vera and her parents went to Karlovy Vary, Eva had to come along.

Eva was the same height as Vera with an oval face, white skin, and   jet-black hair.

Karlovy Vary was a famous Bohemian spa in Europe, considered the place to go for vacation. It was named for the Holy Roman Emperor and Bohemian King Charles IV.

According to legend, in1358 Charles IV was on a hunting expedition when up from the ground came a-bubbling water. Charles decided to built a small castle in that area, naming the town that evolved around it Karlovy

Vary, which means "Charles Boiling Place."

In 1522, the first spa building was built and before long notables like Albrecht of Wallenstein, Peter the Great, and later Bach, Chopin, Beethoven, Freud, and Karl Marx all came to Karlovy Vary. It was a place where royalty, the rich and famous came from all over Europe for treatment.

The first evening they were at Karlovy Vary, Eva and Vera obtained tickets to go to the Carlsbad Town Theatre for the opening night of Mozart's opera "La Noche di Figaro." It was a sold-out gala event, attended by many ambassadors and ministers of foreign affairs.

Vera was wearing a simple but elegant black Coco Chanel dress, matching handbag and gloves, almost no makeup, only blood-red lipstick.

Eva also wore a black cocktail dress and a large pearl necklace.

They were standing in the entry hall when Vera noticed a tall handsome man with green bedroom eyes, black hair, and a great smile.

Vera and that handsome man flirted with each other for a brief moment. "Eva, look at that young man over there—he is so good looking. I wonder who he is."

"I have seen his picture in the social columns of the newspapers. His name is Harold and his father is the ambassador from Brazil."

All of a sudden, all the lights started to flicker.

"Let's go to our seats." Eva grabbed Vera's elbow and they walked to their box seats. Vera was so beautiful that men gasped to see her as she made her way toward the box seats.

Vera sat in her seat dreaming about Harold's beautiful bedroom eyes when she noticed him sitting just below their box.

Harold was looking at her.

Vera gave him a quick smile and pretended to be glancing around the theater.

Suddenly the theater went quiet.

Vera glanced at Harold.

The music started.

Harold looked up at Vera.

The audience applauded.

Vera's eyes met his.

The curtain went up.

Harold gave Vera a warm smile.

A blonde diva walked onto the stage.

Harold and Vera continued staring at each other.

Applause.

Vera smiled at Harold.

Another exquisite actress entered the stage.

Harold smiled back at Vera.

The blonde diva stared her first aria.

Harold and Vera continued looking at each other, each feeling a physical attraction for the other.

The blonde diva finished singing.

Vera smiled flirtatiously at Harold.

The audience applauded.

Harold bowed to Vera.

'Bravo! Bravissima!"

Vera returned the bow to Harold.

The blonde diva bows again.

Harold mouthed to Vera, "You are so beautiful."

More applause.

Vera smiled and mouthed, "Thank you."

The second singer started her song.

Harold and Vera continued flirting with each other.

The opening act ended.

As they were exiting the theater, they ran into Thomas, an organist friend of Eva's. They decided to walk back to the Pupp Hotel to have a drink. Vera looked around hoping to run into Harold; she couldn't get him out of her mind.

While they were having a drink together, Thomas waved to a friend. "Harold, come over here and let me introduce you to Eva and Vera."

Vera turned around, looked over her shoulder, and there he was, the handsome, tall man with the emerald green eyes.

She gave him a warm and seductive smile.

Harold looked at Vera and thought to himself, *She's simply stunning!*

"So nice meeting you," he said without taking his eyes away from Vera.

"How did you like the opera?" Vera asked him. She was immediately attracted to him.

"Oh, I loved it. Mozart is one of my favorite composers and 'La Noche di Figaro' is one of my favorite operas. It is Mozart's most perfectly balanced comedy, with the most beautiful music. It is the most emotionally stirring   opera I have seen. It touched my soul. Don't you agree?" Harold asked, without taking his eyes from Vera.

"Yes, I agree, each movement was meticulously crafted and full of meaning, both on the surface and well below."

"That's right, his music cleverly described all the political turmoil going on during that time..." said Harold.

"Many of those political conflicts are communicated through dance   music in 'La Noche di Figaro,'" Vera said, finishing his sentence.

"Very, Very...Very impressive," said Harold. "You're not just a pretty face, are you?"

Vera smiled.

"This play was considered the guide of the French Revolution, as it clearly shows the struggle between classes." Vera paused. "The play was actually banned from performance in many European countries."

"Mozart himself was a great aficionado of the dance and was known as an exceptional dancer himself," Harold said with a smile.

"I've adored his music ever since I was a little boy."

"I hope you don't take this the wrong way but I was admiring your beauty when I saw you earlier." Harold reached out and touched her face.

"Oh, stop it! You are making me blush. To be honest, I was admiring your beautiful green eyes," Vera said as she laughed.

"Would you like to go for a walk?" Vera asked Harold.

"That would be lovely," Harold quickly replied.

They left Thomas and Eva back in the hotel.

As they walked around the city, fog surrounded them, giving a mysterious and romantic feeling. The fog was created when the cold waters of the Tepla River entered the hot springs.

"Did you know that there are more than sixty hot springs and twelve spas in Karlovy Vary?" Vera asked Harold.

"Karlovy Vary became very popular when people

started drinking the waters and using them as a cleansing cure for different diseases. The combination of different minerals, carbonic and alkaline waters, and the variance in temperature, supposedly creates the healing power of the waters. The Thermal Spring became the place to come for the aristocracy, the European cultural elite."

"Unfortunately, Karlovy Vary is no longer where the European cultural elite come, as it is becoming too commercialized."

"But you are here so there is some aristocracy," Harold said.

"Yes, and don't you forget it," Vera replied, laughing.

"Can you believe that the Czechs have now discovered another version of drinking this mineral water? It is called Becherovka. It is actually a hearty herb and mineral liqueur," she said with a laugh. "It is called our thirteenth spa."

"Oh really?" Harold could not help staring at her.

"Are you even listening to what I'm saying? Why are you staring at me?" Vera gave a nervous laugh.

"You are perfection in this moonlight coming through this fog." Harold said in a whispering voice.

"Oh...stop that!" Vera always felt uncomfortable with compliments. But at the same time, she could feel a very strong desire pulling her closely to him.

"What was I saying?" Vera was blushing.

Both of them could feel a strong carnal desire pulling them closer. They had never experienced this before. Their inner souls were on fire every time they came close to each other.

"Stop staring!" Vera covered her face with her hands and started laughing like an innocent little girl.

"Here to the right is the St. Linhart's Romanesque Chapel. It is the oldest Carlsbad building, going back to 1246."

As they entered Krále Jiřího Avenue, they stood in front of Saints Peter and Paul's Orthodox Church.

"This five-dome edifice was built with the financial help of Russian aristocracy and resembles the design of the Byzantine-Russian church in Ostankino near Moscow."

"Come on, follow me." Vera laughed and ran around the corner.

As Harold turned the corner, he was now at the Kostelní Square. Vera had already managed to find an open door and was entering St. Mary Magdalene's Church. When Harold entered the church, Vera pointed to the two beautiful Gothic Madonna statues. The one to the right side of the church was a baroque altar sculpture by J. Eberl, and on the opposite side was St. Mary Magdalene.

"You are wrong—there are three Madonnas in this church...You are the third Madonna. Have I told you how beautiful you are?"

"Oh no! Not again," Vera said as she walked out of the church.

"Well, Harold, here we are," Vera said as they arrived at the Grand Hotel Pupp where she was staying.

They stood in front of the hotel staring at each other. They were totally attracted to each other but each was too afraid to make the first move.

"It was very nice meeting you," she said, as she extended her hand to say good-bye.

Harold grabbed her hand and pulled her close to him.

"Can I see you tomorrow?" he asked.

"Unfortunately, I am going back to Prague tomorrow morning," she said, as she moved closer to him.

"What? No, you cannot! You must stay! I insist! Please." There was an urgent tone in his voice.

"I must return home. There is a big party in Prague that I must attend. My parents and everyone in Prague will be there. I cannot miss it—my mother would kill me." She smiled.

"Wait! Why don't you come to the party with me? It is going to be held at the *Pražský hrad* Palace."

"Really? I will go with you but there is one condition."

Vera was staring into his eyes as she said, softly, "What's that?"

"Come and dine with me before the party."

Vera nodded her head yes. She was looking at Harold's sensual lips. She wanted so badly to kiss them, she was trembling inside.

Harold caressed Vera's face. Her skin was very soft, her lips were so inviting. That touch drew him close to ecstasy. He turned around and his lips touched hers.

They started kissing passionately. They could feel the heat rising through their bodies, a sexual tension that was building between them.

Both of them could feel it, a desire to explore each other's body.

They stopped as their bodies were trembling with anticipation, a desire they had never experienced before.

"I will see you tomorrow night," Harold said with a big smile.

"Wait, I must give you my address." Vera started laughing.

"That's right."

VII

Kladno, Czechoslovakia

Babushka opened the front door to let Harold into the foyer. She didn't know one word of English and kept talking to Harold in Czech.

He kept smiling at her.

Harold's understanding of Czech was almost non-existent but once in awhile he was able to understand a word or two.

By the time they walked upstairs, he was able to translate two of her sentences.

One she kept saying repeatedly was, "Oh, you probably don't understand what I am saying."

The second sentence he understood had something to do with vodka and happiness.

Meanwhile Vera was upstairs getting ready...

We need a bigger bathroom, there is no room in here, Vera said to herself as she took one more final look in the mirror.

The bathroom included an individual sink, a separate small counter, and one traditional cast iron tub. The shower was a gas tub; one would have to turn on the gas and light the pilot to generate hot water.

It had a gooseneck faucet, the type that is a hand-held shower and looks like a telephone receiver.

Harold was standing in front of the fireplace when Vera walked downstairs.

On the mantel above the fireplace, there was a bust painting of a very beautiful blonde woman looking like a goddess. On each side of the mantel, there was an exquisite Czech red crystal vase.

Harold was wearing a white tuxedo jacket, black tuxedo pants, and a white shirt with a black bow tie. His black hair was gelled back, accentuating his emerald green eyes.

As Vera walked into the living room, Harold turned around and looked at her, mesmerized by her flawless beauty.

It was love at first sight.

She was so exquisitely beautiful with her long eyelashes, her eyebrows plucked into perfect arches, full lips, high cheekbones, and her blonde hair pulled up.

"Good evening! Don't you look handsome," she said, with her dazzling smile.

"Me? Look at you! You look like a movie star," he told her as she giggled.

Vera was wearing the most exquisite and sensual midnight-blue backless gown clinging provocatively to her curves, long black gloves, and black high heel shoes. Her dress had just the right amount of cleavage that her father would not be able to disapprove of it.

A three-carat Van Cleef & Arpels pear-shaped diamond necklace with blue sapphires and a pair of Cartier diamond chandelier earrings with aquamarine drops framed her perfect face and flawless skin.

"Don't you start with me again," she said with an innocent laugh.

Vera turned and looked at Babushka sitting in the chair sipping her vodka. "I can see you made someone very happy and you have a friend for life." Vera giggled.

"My parents apologize for not being here to greet you but they are running late. You will meet at the party."

"Not to worry." Harold smiled.

"Are you hungry?" he asked her. "I made a reservation at this small restaurant in Prague."

"Yes, I'm starving," Vera replied.

As they were walking out of the living room, Babushka rose slowly from her chair, hugged Harold, and said something in Czech.

He smiled.

"She said that you are a fine young man and she thanks you for the vodka. You made an old lady very happy," Vera translated.

They all laughed.

In Prague, they went to a very small exclusive fourteenth-century Gothic restaurant located on the island in the Vltava River. They sat outside on the open terrace, there were candles everywhere, making it a very cozy and romantic restaurant.

To the right they could see the Opera House and the old town. To the left they had a magnificent panoramic view of the Petrin Hill with the castle at the top.

They ordered Beluga caviar to start, followed by filet mignon wrapped in pastry with sauce, perigoundine, and knedliky, famous Czech dumplings.

The food was superb.

Harold raised his glass of Dom Perignon and made a toast, "Here is to the beginning of a very enchanted evening."

"Yes, to a perfect evening." Vera smiled seductively as she stared into his eyes.

Part of her felt like a young woman with sexual desires that made her feel on fire. She was so attracted to him, to his nice smile, to his beautiful eyes. The woman inside of her wanted him.

Harold's attention was totally turned to her. His eyes were fixed on her, his stare was one of desire.

She was having such a marvelous time, it felt just like a dream.

After dinner, Vera ordered some Turecka kava.

Vera asked Harold, "You have had Turkish coffee

before, right?"

"Humm, but of course." He smiled.

Vera smiled back, wondering if he was telling the truth.

Five minutes later, after they started drinking their coffee, Harold asked her, "What is all this in my coffee?"

Vera started to laugh, "I knew it—you've never had Turkish coffee before, have you?"

Harold was blushing and trying to clear his mouth, Vera was laughing uncontrollably. His mouth was full of coffee grounds.

"When drinking Turkish coffee you need to know when to stop swallowing the coffee. You need to stop drinking before you disturb the deposit of coffee grounds in the bottom of the cup."

"You knew this was going to happen, didn't you?" Harold asked, laughing.

Vera couldn't stop laughing.

Harold was staring at her, mystified by her beauty and sense of style.

Vera grinned. She looked at her watch, an elegant stainless-steel model with a row of tiny diamonds around the face. She took a deep breath and said, "We better be going to the party. It is eight fifty."

VIII

As they were approaching the castle, they could see the cars lined up to get into *Pražský hrad,* the Prague Castle, one of the biggest castles in the world.

Part of the street was barricaded to make way for the chauffeured Mercedes sedans, limousines, and luxury cars so they could roll through the gates and continue down the driveway into a sweeping circular driveway.

There was a barrage of photographers in front of the castle, waiting to take pictures of those entering the party.

The forty-foot-high marble entrance hall was filled with European nobility, high society, and socialites.

As they left the car and Harold was straightening his jacket, someone asked Vera, "Aren't you going to introduce us?"

"But of course! Good evening, Countess Ondracek," Vera said politely as she pulled Harold toward her. "Let me introduce to Harold Coimbra, the son of the Brazilian ambassador to Czechoslovakia. Harold, please meet Countess Ondracek."

"It is my pleasure, Countess Ondracek," Harold said politely as he bent over and kissed her hand. He was the perfect gentleman.

"What a charming young man, and so good looking. Veruska, let me look at you. You look so beautiful," 51

Countess Ondracek continued, looking at both of them.

"Thank you," Vera said graciously as she turned to Harold and asked, "Well, are you ready? This is going to be interesting evening for you." Vera paused for a second. "Hopefully it will not be too painful."

"Don't worry, everything will be fine, the most important thing is that I'm here next to you. I probably will be very amused." Harold whispered in her ear.

Vera's hand touched Harold's hand and there was an immediate burning desire to kiss him.

As they were making their way through the entrance hall, people started   coming up to Vera. Harold found himself being very amused by the endless hellos. "Darling! How are you?" a woman said as she kissed Vera's cheeks.

"Moi? At home? Darling, I wouldn't miss this soiree for anything!"

"You look so Bee-you-tee-ful tonight!" a blonde girl said, while she was looking at Harold.

"You look marvelousssss..." another girl said, with such an insincere tone of voice.

"You look so Garbo-esque..."

Vera turned and looked at Harold who had a grin in his face.

They couldn't keep themselves from laughing.

Vera felt so happy being next to Harold.

He could not help but he fascinated with her.

"Well, well, look who is here!"

Vera turned and looked at Eva and Thomas. "How are you?"

"We are fine, how are the two lovebirds?" Eva responded quickly.

"Who? Us?" Vera's face turned bright red.

"Isn't this a great party?" Harold said, trying to change the subject.

"Yes. This is the social event!"

"Too bad certain people are invited to this party, like Thorna. She has been saying some wicked and nasty things about us," said Eva.

"Personally, I find all this gossiping very annoying and intolerable." Vera looked up, turning her nose in the air, and using a very sophisticated and sarcastic voice while taking a puff of her cigarette in its holder.

They couldn't help themselves, as they started to laugh.

Thorna was an American woman living in Prague, the perfect nouveau riche. She was a size sixteen black woman, squashed into size ten leopard-print dress. The weird thing was that, in her own way, she looked rather good in the animal print.

"Thorna's conversation and preoccupation are so unimportant." Vera sighed, and continued, "She is always giving everyone her unwelcome advice, always showing an expression of superiority on her fat face."

"There aren't too many people that can put up with such a nightmare," Eva said. "She is an aficionado of nothing."

They all laughed.

"She is just jealous, after all," Eva concluded.

"I have to go and find my parents so they can meet Harold." Vera said as she grabbed Harold's hand.

"Ahhh! Not serious? Meeting the parents already?" Eva smiled.

"Eva, sometimes you are as annoying as a real sister," Vera said and smiled.

"I have no idea of what you are talking about," Eva said innocently.

"Will we see you later? Or are you taking off like you did last night?" Thomas asked.

Vera and Harold looked at each other and smiled.

From there they walked up the grand marble stairway.

As they reached the end of the staircase Vera asked, "Are you ready to meet my parents?"

Vera took Harold's hand again and led him to her parents as he smiled at them.

Vera could feel her own heart pounding.

Her mother stood, erect and elegant, wearing a long

black velvet dress and long black gloves. She wore her hair up and had sparkling jewelry around her neck. She had dark, piercing eyes with heavy arched eyebrows above them, full firmly closed lips, and her hair was drawn smoothly over the forehead—altogether a strikingly beautiful woman.

Vladimir was standing on her right wearing a long black dinner jacket, black pants, and a white shirt with a bow tie.

As Vera introduced Harold to her mother, he smiled and said, "Ah! Now I know where Vera gets her exquisite looks. It is so very nice meeting you." He bent over to kiss her hand.

Harold started talking to Vera's mother, completely captivating her attention. They talked of art, music, and architecture.

Vera could tell her mother was very impressed with Harold's knowledge of so much culture and by his sophistication.

Vera noticed several times, that Harold's eyes were fixed on her while he was talking to her mother.

Meanwhile Vera walked toward Vladimir, kissed him quickly, and asked, "Father, are you enjoying the party?"

"But of course!" Vladimir replied.

When Harold approached Vera's father, Vladimir asked, "So you are the son of the Brazilian ambassador? The one that everyone is talking about?"

"I'm afraid so, Dr. Pisova," Harold replied and laughed.

Vladimir laughed lightly.

Her mother took Vera's hand and whispered, "What a charming young man, so likable and polite and very good looking."

"I'm glad you approve." Vera smiled.

Harold turned to Vera's mother and Vladimir. "I love your country, the history, and the culture. Prague is probably the most beautiful city I ever seen." Harold paused for a second and smiled at them. "The unique combination of architecture and design mixture such as Romanesque, Gothic, baroque, Art Nouveau, Cubism, and functionalism all play a role in the city's amazing display of well-preserved architecture making this city such a unique city."

Vera grinned. "Are you ready to go to the ballroom?"

"Sure let's go…Oh, Mrs. Pisova, please make sure to save a dance for me."

"I will."

As they started to walk away, Vera turned around and noticed her mother and Vladimir exchanging glances and smiling to each other.

The top floor corridor was wide, leading toward the ballroom. Approaching the ballroom they could hear the orchestra playing and the voices getting louder. The two gigantic doors leading into the ballroom were open, and on each side of the entrance, were handsome fair-haired identical twin boys dressed alike. They were handing masks to each guest, black masks to the men, and white masks to women. Inside the door was a pair of gorgeous identical twin blonde-haired girls serving champagne to the quests. They were dressed like Venus, the Roman goddess of love and beauty.

Along the wall to the left of the doors was a sage with a stone replica on the Cathedrale d'image in southern France.

Dancers were performing a scenic flashback of moments of a human life, an unconventional combination of film projection, music, choreography, and acrobatic fairy tale, making it a very exotic dance piece.

On the opposite side of the ballroom was a small all-girl band. All the girls looked exactly the same. They were wearing white tuxedos and white high heels, no shirts under the tuxedo jackets, just a black leather necklace with diamonds. A black stripe painted across their eyes gave them a very sensual and intriguing look.

The ballroom walls were covered with black silk fabric, and lanterns hanging on the walls provided a low lighting, making everything look very mysterious.

In the center of the dance floor there was a waterfall in a pond. The bottom of the pond was all glass and under the glass was a burning fire. The soft light from the fire was reflected through the blue waters of the pound.

Right next to the pond there was a waterfall. Behind the waterfall was a twenty-foot-diameter pool of ice. Inside the pool were layers of colored ice: dark blue and bright yellow-colored crystals. Everything looked so magical.

Harold could feel the eyes of others measuring them, particularly when Vera walked across the room; everyone was looking at her. She embodied grace, charm, sensuality, and a true ladylike attitude.

"Come on, let's dance."

Harold walked to the center of the polished floor and extended his hand, waiting for Vera to join him.

White rose petals covered the entire dance floor.

As that moment, Vera realized everybody was staring at both of them.

She walked slowly across the dance floor with the confidence of a woman accustomed to the gaze of men.

Harold put his arm around her and started guiding her body into his. It was just the two of them dancing, and they looked marvelous together.

"This is a lovely song," Vera said.

Strangers in the night exchanging glances
Wondering in the night

Veruska

Imagining you in love with me
Time just forgot to exist
And it lets me spend
Light years alone with you.

Their bodies were moving like one, very sensually and gracefully. Vera was so happy staring into Harold's eyes while he was holding her very closely to him.

Lovers at first sight,
I whisper you name
And like magic, you appeared.

Harold knew men around them were watching with jealous eyes.

They danced totally unaware of anybody else.

"Do you realize you are the most beautiful woman here?" Harold whispered softly into her ear.

After dancing for a few hours, Vera and Harold decided to get some fresh air. They went through the French doors, walking out on the graveled terrace in front of the majestic facade of the castle.

Once they reached the end of the terrace, they walked down several steps that led them into beautiful gardens surrounding the castle.

"This is the first of three Castle courtyards."

Harold put his arm around Vera.

Below, they could see the entire city. The sky was clear and the full moon was out making the view spectacular and romantic.

"Look, over there is where we had dinner next to the *Karlův most, the* Charles Bridge with its thirty baroque statues and three towers, going across the Vltava River," Vera whispered.

The picturesque city skyline was breathtaking with all the uncountable towers, turrets, and steeples from all the great churches and palaces.

Harold couldn't take his eyes off her, and he looked into her eyes and said, "You are an angel!"

They kissed passionately.

Slowly, they started walking into the Royal Garden; the silence was broken only by the noise of their feet walking on top of the pebbles below.

"Did you know that this castle is one of the largest castles in the world?" Vera asked Harold.

"The largest?" Harold replied.

"Are you making fun of me?" Vera asked, making a sad face.

"Me? Never," Harold said with a grin.

They walked under the Royal Gazebo and found themselves looking at a very exotic landscape with beautiful cedar and fig trees and tulips.

Vera pointed to the tulips and said, "Legend says that the tulips were a gift from a Turkish ambassador who introduced the red, white, and yellow tulips into Europe. The tulips bloomed in the Castle Royale Garden for the first time anywhere in Europe, long before spreading across the European continent, in particular Holland."

She looked at the stars above as she felt a warm breeze on her face. For the first time in her life, she was happy and content.

Harold slipped behind her and his fingers started caressing her face. The caressing of his fingers and the small kisses on her neck unleashed an incredible carnal desire. Vera tried to free herself by pulling away but she was completely helpless.

She cursed him because she liked being in control. She wanted him as much as he wanted her.

Harold's hands could not stop caressing her.

She stared into his eyes for a moment, as his hands ran through her hair.

"Thank you for making this evening so special," Vera whispered in his ear.

All of a sudden, Vera felt his tongue gently forcing her mouth open before he started to kiss her passionately.

When they stopped kissing, Vera opened her eyes. Harold was staring at her so intently, as if she was a magnificent work of art.

Vera gave him a very innocent smile. That smile was a smile that he would remember forever.

The party lasted till dawn.

IX

The following morning, Harold and Vera met in front of the castle. They planned to spend the day together exploring the beautiful city of Prague.

Vera looked so radiant, her skin was perfect, and she was glowing with happiness. She was wearing a white cotton dress, dark glasses, and her hair was pulled back.

Harold was very excited, not only about spending time with her but also being able to explore places where Wolfgang Amadeus Mozart had been when he was in Prague.

Harold had on his round turtle dark glasses, and his black hair was gelled back. He wore a V-neck sweater and a stripe-on-stripe cotton shirt.

"Good morning! I cannot get over on how beautiful you are. Every time I see you, you look more beautiful than before," Harold said as he kissed her.

"Are you still drunk from last night?" Vera asked, laughing.

"No, I'm not! I just can't get over how beautiful you are and how lucky I am being with you." He smirked. "Anyway in our walk today can we make sure to stop at a few places. You know that Mozart is my favorite composer and I found out a few places where he stayed when he was here in Prague." He paused. "Can we start here at the Strahov

Monastery?" Harold asked, pointing to the building west of the castle.

"Sure." Vera replied.

"While walking the neighborhood with Josefina Dušek, Mozart visited the Strahov Monastery, which is famous for its musical tradition and its   first-rate organ. Mozart ended up playing the organ. According to Norbert Lehmann, the organist who was present at the time, Mozart developed a theme for a fugue from Brixi´s Requiem in C minor in a totally new manner and so skillfully that it left everybody in a state of euphoria."

After looking at the organ, they looked at the ornate library halls and the frescoes in the Theological Hall.

Then they decided to walk through the forest below the castle. The sky was clear. They were looking at the incredible view of the castle and the entire city as they enjoyed the sunshine.

When Harold took Vera's hand, both of them could feel the energy between them. They couldn't get enough of each other.

Harold was staring at Vera, her hair fallen over her face—she looked so angelic.

Vera was so excited and happy to be with Harold. Everything was so magical.

They started walking down the hill, through the

crooked alleyways of Nový Svet, making their way toward the Charles Bridge.

As Nový Svet is known for having some spectacular secret private gardens, they would go around and try opening some of the gates leading to the gardens hidden behind high walls.

"Look! Here is St. Nicholas Church. Did you know that there were more than four thousand mourners at this church paying respect after Mozart died?" Harold asked Vera.

She was smiling. "Oh really?" Vera replied sarcastically.

"Now, who is making fun of whom?" Harold grabbed Vera and started tickling her.

"No, stop! Please, stop!" Vera said, laughing like a small girl.

"OK, but you better behave or otherwise my fingers will come and tickle you again," Harold said as his fingers moved up and down in a ticklish movement.

"Where was I? Oh yes, Prague was Mozart's second home; he was better received in Prague than in Vienna. After his death it was Prague that honored him by having a great funeral mass in St. Nicholas Church."

That afternoon Harold turned to Vera and said, "Oh, by the way, I have a little surprise for you."

"I love surprises! What is it?" Vera asked.

"You will see."

He found a grove of trees below the castle, took Vera by the hand, and led her to a nice spot. He pulled a blanket from under one of the bushes, spread it out, and motioned to Vera to lie on it.

It was still a beautiful afternoon, sunny with a few rain clouds floating in the blue sky.

"Now close your eyes and no peeking."

Harold got up and walked toward another bush where he had hidden a picnic basket. He took out the linen, silverware, and the champagne glasses.

He placed one arm around Vera's waist, drawing her close to him. The warm sunlight felt very nice on their skin.

He set everything up. "I hope you like what I brought...we have champagne, pate, shrimp cocktail, chicken, roast beef, different types of gourmet cheeses, and fruit. Is this OK? You may open your eyes now."

Vera opened her eyes and looked at the display, "This is so wonderful, just perfect." Vera's eyes were getting teary.

"You are perfection!" Harold said as he kept staring at her.

Vera blushed.

"Let's open the champagne and start eating."

They stayed there for a few hours flirting with each

other, kissing, and rolling around the blanket, feeling the heat of their bodies. They could feel the sexual tension increasing between them. They laughed and talked about everything important to them. Both of them were very happy.

"Look over there!" Vera said as she got up and pointed down to the statue of St. John of Nepomuk. It was raining above the Charles Bridge and a rainbow ended right behind that statue.

"That statue is the oldest on the bridge," Vera continued. "It portrays scenes from the life of St. John of Nepomuk, including the confession of Queen Johanna and the saint's death. According to legend, St. John of Nepomuk was thrown from the bridge into the river where he drowned. If you touch the statue it will bring you good fortune and ensure your return to the city of Prague."

"Well that is one place we need to stop so I can touch the statue. Then you will know that I will be back." Harold smiled seductively.

"The rainbow leading to that statue is a sign that we are meant to be   together," Harold told Vera as he looked into her eyes.

He leaned toward her and started kissing her, igniting full carnal desire between them.

Vera's body was trembling with anticipation and desire.

"I've had a bit too much champagne—you better look

out." Vera laughed.

Vera could feel his lips touching hers. The fire was erupting inside her, a burning desire. She could feel his excitement.

How long it will take until we lose control? I want him so badly. Vera thought to herself.

Both knew they could not control their desire any longer.

Suddenly it began to rain.

They got up, bundled everything, and ran for cover.

It was dark by the time they came down the hill and walked across the Charles Bridge. The fog was intense, creating a sinister and romantic atmosphere. Every time they walked by one of the sculpted saints it looked like it was pointing or warning them against the darkening skies surrounding them.

Harold had his arm around Vera.

"In an ideal world everyone would meet the love of their life, fall in love, get married, be happy and in love and live happily for the rest of their life." Vera smiled seductively. "But reality is that you go through one big love, things don't work out, your expectations are reduced, and that is when you start getting an idea of what you can expect realistically."

"You are too young to have such a pessimistic idea about love."

"Am I being pessimistic or just being realistic?" Vera

smirked.

"Have you ever been in love before?" Harold asked.

"Me? In love? I don't think so. I dated and had feelings toward Count Rafaello Ondracek, the son of Countess Ondracek. You remember her, don't you? She was one of the first people you met last night when we arrived at the castle."

"Oh, yes, I remember. Trust me, when you fall in love, you will know it. You will not say 'I don't think so,'" Harold said, with a loving smile on his face.

"Hummm, I guess you are right." Vera smiled back at him.

"I'm always right...don't you forget that!" Harold said, laughing out loud.

"We'll see if that is true or just a Harold perception."

"You will see." Harold winked.

"Until a woman knows who she really is and until she is happy with herself there is no way a man can fall in love with her," Harold said as he grabbed Vera's hand.

"I've never been so happy in my life," Vera replied, softly.

They were engulfed by an emotion and desire they had never felt before.

"Look, here we are!" Harold turned around and walked toward the statue of St. John of Nepomuk, closed his eyes and rubbed his hand on the statue.

"Now you know I will be back again to see you."

Vera nodded. "I hope so."

They started to kiss passionately, before they continued walking and holding each other.

A few minutes later, they were in front of the Orloj, the astronomical clock.

"According to legend," Vera explained, "Hanuk, the master who built this fascinating clock that gives you the time, the position of the sun and the moon, and shows saints' days, calendar and zodiac signs, was blinded by the city fathers so he could not build another clock like this one."

They continue walking through the silent city, holding hands, walking through the courtyards as their footsteps echoed in the darkness.

"Look, here is where Mozart stayed." Harold pointed to a building. "During his first visit when he was premiering his new opera, "Don Giovanni," he lodged here at the pub at the Uhelný trh near the Nostitz Theatre."

"You really know everything about Mozart, don't you?" Vera rested her head on his shoulder. She was wishing that the feeling of happiness she was experiencing would never end.

X

After their all-day walk, they went back to Harold's apartment.

It was a very spacious two-bedroom apartment in a building that had once been a big house belonging to a Czech baron.

He went into the kitchen for ice.

Vera was standing in front of the fireplace, her back turned away from the balcony. She was mesmerized by the fire and thinking what a great day it had been.

Harold returned silently into the room.

The light from the fireplace was shining through her white cotton dress, accentuating her silhouette, softly caressing the curves of her sensual and perfect body.

He put his arms around her.

The sexual tension between their bodies generated heat that pulled their bodies together.

His hands pulled her body closer to his as he started kissing her neck.

Vera moaned with pleasure. Her heart was beating wildly.

Then his moist lips moved closer to her lips.

She shut her eyes as his lips touched hers. His tongue

parted her lips. He could feel his eyelashes rubbing against her face.

He undid the clasps of her cotton dress and slowly it fell around her. He lifted her body and gently lowered it to the floor in front of the fireplace. Her body was so warm.

She felt her teeth clench with anticipation and desire—she wanted him so badly.

Vera ripped away Harold's shirt while undoing his pants.

There was no hair in his chest. Her hands were trembling.

His tongue started exploring every inch of her body, starting at her toes and gradually working his way up her long and slender legs.

The curves of her sensual body were being caressed by the soft light from the fireplace, the same perfection as the curves and shadows of the beach sands during a beautiful sunset.

Harold could smell her perfume.

He kissed her between her tights as her legs came slowly apart as her desire for him exploded inside of her.

Vera couldn't help but moan and grind her teeth with pleasure.

Harold was looking up, staring into her eyes, mesmerized by her beauty.

The hours of foreplay turned into minutes of pleasure and desire.

They could feel their bodies getting wet from the moisture generated by the passionate heat coming from their bodies.

Harold saw the face of an innocent girl turning into the face of a woman full of carnal and sexual desire.

Her hair fell over his naked body and Harold couldn't get enough of her naked sensuality.

Both of them started to lose control, as passion and desire were taking over their bodies and their minds.

Harold slowly got in top of her...his hands holding her hands above her head as her hair covered part of her face.

Their eyes were looking at each other.

His body was pinned against hers, and he had such an urge to take her.

Vera whispered in his ear, "Take me! Now! I'm yours."

It happened so quickly...he was inside of her and both bodies were riding as one.

Harold felt his teeth clench with pleasure.

They were moaning until they reached a climax.

Finally, Harold's body fell to the side as each tried to stop trembling with such great pleasure.

Their hearts were beating so fast they kept gasping for more air.

Sweat was dripping from their faces; they could feel its salty taste.

As Vera opened her eyes she saw Harold staring at

her. She was feeling happiness as she smiled at him.

It was the most overpowering experience either had ever known; they were too dazed to speak. They were just staring and holding each other.

Everything was beautiful and they were so happy together, exhausted, and soaking wet.

When Harold opened his eyes, he saw Vera staring at the fire.

"Are you all right, my darling?" he asked, as his fingers caressed her face.

"I'm happier than I ever been," she mumbled, her face full of passion.

"Are you tired?" Harold asked.

"Not really...I am ready for the second round!" Vera said as she moved on top of Harold.

"Why are you staring?" she asked.

"Because right now you are a vision of perfection...your face, your naked body."

"Oh, stop it! You are drunk!" Vera laughed.

"No!" Harold said as he pulled her toward him and his lips touched hers.

Suddenly, their bodies became entangled as one and they were rolling around on the floor in front of the fireplace. His tongue was going up and down her body.

Vera could not stop him; she wanted more and more.

She would try stopping him but her body was inviting

him in, as she moaned very softly.

Passion and desire were consuming both of them again.

By the time Vera got up, it was almost morning. She got dressed silently and made her way down the dark hall.

XI

The following five days were the happiest days that Vera and Harold had ever experienced.

They would spend hour after hour talking intensely, sharing their most intimate secrets.

They would look at the medieval buildings and point out unique sculptures used to decorated the façade of those buildings such as the saintly statues or the Black Madonna in her gilded cage. They would go for long walks in the woods below the castle, where they would admire the majestic city's skyline, eat some cheese with apples, and sip wine. They would walk down the banks of the Vltava River or visit the Troja Chateau, considered Prague's Versailles castle.

Harold was the most wonderful man she had ever known. Everything was perfect and romantic.

Vera would close her eyes, trying to remember every second that she was with Harold. She wanted to remember the feeling of happiness when they were laughing, having an Irish coffee at the Brno Caffe, and the way his lips felt when they were kissing.

The day that Vera and Harold were regretting the most had arrived, Harold's last night in Czechoslovakia.

After dinner, they took a long walk through the city, walking down the narrow cozy streets, holding each other, looking at the eclectic buildings, great churches, and palaces.

It was their last night together and they were trying to make the most of it, enjoying every second. They were together, lying on the floor of Harold's empty apartment. His furniture had been shipped to Italy. The only things left in his apartment were a blanket, two pillows, a few candles, two wine glasses, and a bottle of wine.

The candlelight was reflecting on her fine blonde hair, which was like silk floating around her face. Her lips were wet and shining, she had a seductive smile on her face.

Her body quivered as she tried to suppress her feeling of desire, but she wanted him so badly.

They held each other very tightly.

Harold was silent, just staring at Vera.

"What's the matter?" Vera asked him.

He said very softly, "We'll never be able to be just friends."

Vera turned pale.

"Harold," Vera said in a low and disappointed voice, "do you seriously mean that you believe friendship between us is impossible?"

Harold took a deep breath before answering her.

"Yes." His voice was trembling.

"Don't you see?" He paused. "It is impossible! It is impossible because I fallen in love with you!"

Vera smiled. "My darling, don't you know that I am also in love with you?" Her voice broke down for a quick second.

Vera was totally in ecstasy lying in Harold's strong arms. She had never been so happy, and she didn't want to think about tomorrow.

He held her in a long, tight embrace, giving her long passionate kisses, which told her of his devotion.

There, in the shadow, they whispered their love and their devotion for each other.

The next morning came and Harold was gone.

The following months were unbearable, as Vera missed Harold very much.

Vera tried making the best of the situation. The vivid memories of the ten days she and Harold had spent together and her fantasizing about the day they would be reunited were the only two things that kept her from falling apart. Her life became a dull, tedious routine.

Babushka was not only Vera's favorite relative, but she was the one that Vera turned to for advice.

Vera felt comfortable pouring out her feelings and fears because Babushka was one of those rare people who always accepted you for who you were; she never passed judgment on anyone.

Her advice was always great advice so Babushka was the one who Veruska went to for advice when Harold moved to Italy.

"L'Amour! L'Amour! My little Veruska, first love it is the strongest feeling you will ever have. The intensity of the first love is the strongest you will ever feel." Babushka paused for a second.

"Trust me, if this is your first love then you will meet again. I know every minute you are separated feels like an eternity, one minute without him and you feel as if you have lost everything."

"You feel like you are going to die," Vera said under her breath.

Babushka was the only one who was able to calm Vera down when she would think that Harold had forgotten her because a few weeks had gone by and she hadn't received any letters from him.

Babushka would be the one to remind her. "Let's not jump into any conclusions. Give him some more time. You need to remember that with all the changes happening in our country—such as the expulsion of two and half million Germans, the setting up of the new Communist party, Harold's family settling residency in Italy—the mail could take longer than the normal three-week delivery."

XII

Rome, Italy

Back in Rome, Harold was sitting outside in the garden at the Villa Rafaello, the family estate in the foothill of the Italian Alps, thinking about Veruska.

Harold's family enjoyed a great lifestyle, traveling all over the world and enjoying the elevated social status associated with Martin's position as the ambassador from Brazil. Since an early age Harold was groomed to become a diplomat. He was always polite, well dressed and had impeccable manners. He was raised in a cultured, musical environment and developed a lifelong passion for classical music. Mozart was his favorite classical composer.

Harold closed his eyes and started remembering all the times he had held Vera in his arms, how much he enjoyed her lips touching his, her silky hair brushing against his skin, The fire erupting and the burning desire erupting inside of him.

He wanted to see her again but knew it was impossible, Czechoslovakia was in turmoil, as the Communist Party started to take over the government.

No visas were being granted to travel in or out of the

country.

If you were lucky to receive your mail there was a good possibility it had been opened and read by the authorities. Generally it would take three to four weeks for the mail to be delivered.

Harold was trying to finish writing a letter to Vera telling her about some changes happening in his life

Harold's life was also in turmoil. His parents were getting divorced. His father was being transferred to Washington. Harold was staying in Rome for a few more months, working for the Brazilian embassy.

Ondina, his mother, decided to grant her husband a divorce and she was returning to Florence. She was a very charming and sweat woman, her eyes lighter than his, a sapphire blue, she was slim with black hair and always dressed very elegantly. She was the perfect diplomat's wife, always making sure that the household ran properly and that everything was in perfect condition when they entertained at the villa.

Harold was very close to his mother and he was having a hard time accepting his parents divorce.

Martin, his father, was always too busy being Mr. Ambassador had very little time for his sons.

Harold and his two brothers were not close to him.

Harold started remembering when Martin called him into the library to talk about the divorce. He walked into the library and took the armchair as indicated by his father.

Once he sensed something was wrong, he decided to look out the window.

"My son, please look at me." His father took a deep breath. "I'm your father, look at me!"

Harold continued looking out the window.

"Alright, have it your way."

"Son, are you listening to me?"

Harold didn't move an inch.

"After being together for so many years your mother and I have grown apart." He waited for a second, to see if Harold would say anything. "Unfortunately, these things happen. Don't ask me why?"

"Why?" Harold had suddenly turned and stared at his father.

"Let me tell you why...it is called Shirley...trampy Shirley."

"Enough! I do not want to you to refer to Shirley like that! Have I made myself clear?" Martin's face turned bright red.

"Perfectly, and I don't wish to hear anything about you love affair with her." Harold answered as he turned around and started staring out the window.

"I'm here to tell you that I will always take care and

provide monetary support to your mother and my three sons." His father took a deep breath.

"Perhaps I was not always here for you guys but that doesn't change the fact that I love you and I will always continue loving all of you."

"Lies!" Harold screamed at his father.

Harold remembered the afternoon he came home unexpectedly and found Shirley and his father kissing in the backyard.

He didn't say anything, waited until his father went into the house and then walked outside where Shirley was standing.

"I'm Harold Coimbra." He said, coldly, "and who might you be?"

Harold was stunned to learn that she was just a manicurist. She had grown up as the black sheep of a poor blue collar family. *She must be a gold digger* he thought to himself.

Harold though she was too flirtatious around men. He considered her behavior totally inappropriate for someone accompanying an ambassador.

To make matters worth, his father thought that her flirtation was a way to meet people, it was really fun to be around her.

"Lies," Harold continued yelling at his father. "We were a family until Shirley came into the picture, that gold digger destroyed our family. She isolated and brain washed you."

His father tried reasoning with him, "My son, be reasonable, with or without Shirley my relationship with your mother was over."

Silence.

"Unfortunately these things happen and you cannot say that it was one thing or one person that caused the relationship to end. It was a combination of many factors that made us grow apart." His father looked at him hoping to get some understanding.

"You haven't even tried savaging your marriage." Harold snapped at him.

"Now, that's unfair for you to say! You don't know that. Why do you despise me so much?"

"I do not hate you but I know one thing for sure…I just lost a father!"

"You mark my words! You will never see me again."

"My son please be reasonable…" his father pleaded.

"No! I don't want anything to do with you!" Harold shook his head.

"I feel trapped here. It is time for me to leave."

Harold got up from his chair and walked out.

His father had decided to let some time go by and try later when Harold had more time to think about the matter. Part of Harold's anger was due to the fact that his father wasn't able to get him a visa to go to Czechoslovakia. Although his friend Prime Minister Masaryk's death was ruled an accident he was convinced that he was indeed murdered.

"Can you have the car ready?" Harold's father asked, one of the servants.

"I must go to the airport. I am flying to Brasilia. I have a meeting with the Brazilian President Getúlio Vargas "

"Right away, Ambassador Coimbra," the servant replied.

Harold had finally finished writing the letter to Vera describing everything that had happened since he had left Czechoslovakia.

He wished Vera would be next to him, supporting each other through those difficult times.

XIII

Prague, Czechoslovakia

As Martin had predicted, slowly the Communist Party started a campaign of political agitation and intrigue to gain control of the Czechoslovakian government, Shortly thereafter, Jan Masaryk, the non-Communist foreign minister, was found dead. He was, dressed in his pajamas, in the courtyard of the foreign ministry, below his bathroom window. The initial investigation concluded that he committed suicide by jumping out of the window, although many were convinced that he was thrown out.

The Communist Party quickly staged a coup d'etat, bringing Czechoslovakia under the Iron Curtain, under the domain of the Kremlin. President Edvard Beneš was forced to abdicate.

Czechoslovakia became a Soviet-style state.

A new constitution was enacted, including a program for nationalizing the economy. Gradually the transformation began into a classless society, based upon common ownership of the means of production and the end of private property.

Meanwhile, Harold was traveling back and forth between Italy and Brazil, working for the Brazilian Embassy in Rome.

Veruska

With the changes in Czechoslovakia and Harold's traveling, it was taking months for the letters to reach each other.

Vera was trying to imagine her life without Harold but every time she did, she felt her heart breaking into smaller and smaller pieces.

"Veruska! Veruska, are you ready? Hurry up! We are already late," Vera's mother yelled from the entrance hall.

"I'm coming! Where are we going for lunch with Aunt Maci?" Vera asked.

"We are having lunch at her house, we..."

"At her house! Why are we rushing so much?" Vera asked.

"As I was saying before I was so rudely interrupted, we are having lunch at her house because she also invited two tenants who are renting one of the rooms." Her mother smiled.

"Great, this is going to be such a boring lunch. They are probably a hundred years old," Vera said softly.

"That's not very nice. One day we will all be there."

Vera smiled sweetly.

"Life," her mother whispered, "is full of surprises."

What did she mean by that? Vera asked herself.

Vera and her mother were walking toward the front door when Babushka came out of her room.

"Good morning, Babushka! Are you coming to lunch

with us?"

"Good morning. No thank you, you know that your aunt Maci never serves vodka at lunchtime." Babushka rolled her eyes as she started to go up the staircase.

Aunt Maci lived on Masarykovo Nabrezi Street. Her two-bedroom apartment was close to the Karlova University in Prague, with a beautiful view of the castle and Petrin Hill.

She had a moderate income from her husband's estate on which she was able to live semi-independently.

To supplement her income, she rented the spare bedroom to students at the university.

When they arrived at Aunt Maci's apartment, she was waiting for them at the door and said, impatiently, "You are late."

Vera's mother looked at Veruska as she said, "I know, we are so sorry, traffic was a nightmare."

"Well, the boys have already started eating because they have to return to the university."

"Boys? University?" Veruska asked.

"Yes, they are cousins and students at the university."

"Please do come in."

"Veruska, meet Stephan and George."

"Stephan and George, meet Veruska and her mother, Vera." Aunt Maci smiled.

Stephan was a handsome young man with a five-o'clock shadow, suntanned face, and his brown curly hair was gelled back. He was wearing khaki pants, a tan-green cotton shirt, and big black stomping boots.

Vera could sense that he was a flamboyant type with an attitude of his masculinity and sexuality.

Vera smiled flirtatiously at him.

George, Stephan's cousin, was an average-looking young man, pale, skinny and very shy.

Stephan couldn't take his eyes off Veruska.

"Where are you from?" Vera's mother asked.

"I grew up in Bratislava," Stephan answered.

"I see, a nice Slovak boy...is that were you parents live?"

"My parents used to live there." Stephan's voice saddened.

"Did they move during the war?"

"Mother, please stop asking so many questions." Vera sensed uneasiness in his voice.

"That's all right." Stephan took a deep breath. "You see, my parents were brutally murdered by the Nazis during the war."

There was a moment's hesitation as Stephan's mind was filled with images of his parents.

"I'm so sorry," Vera's mother said.

"My parents and I were in our car heading north away from the city when we were stopped by the Nazi soldiers. They were searching the area for two men and a woman who were responsible for killing two German soldiers that morning. They lined up the cars and asked to see each person's identification card." Stephan took another deep breath before continuing. "Two of the German soldiers approached the car in front of us and asked them a few questions. All of a sudden, one of the armed soldiers pointed his gun at them and yelled, 'You are lying. Step out of the car.' The car in front of us tried taking off, going up and over the curb, and started firing at the German soldiers who fired back at them. My mother grabbed me, put me under the dashboard, and used her body as a shield. Unfortunately, my parents' car was in the way. My parents and the two soldiers were killed by the flying bullets. Someone opened the car door and rescued me before other soldiers arrived at the scene. The Nazis denied killing my parents. They said that my parents were part of the resistance group that killed the two soldiers that morning."

Tears filled Vera's eyes.

"My mom's brother, Tony, looked after me after my parents were killed. He is a simple man, without education, who lives on a small farm just outside of Bratislava."

"Oh, I'm so sorry," Vera's mother said.

Stephan was silent for a moment.

"Don't worry…I was constantly told by some of my uncle's friends that I was unlikely to amount to anything. So one day my cousin, George, and I decided to pack some clothes and took a train to Prague. Once here, we decided to go to the university."

Stephan spent the rest of the lunch talking to Vera. Time went very quickly.

"It is time for us to go back to the university," said George.

"You are right. I must go, and I have to take a test next class," Stephan said as he looked at Vera.

"Au revoir!" Vera smiled sweetly.

"Can I see you again?" asked Stephan.

Vera hesitated before telling him yes.

He smiled. "Good, I will get your number from your aunt."

At first, Vera refused to see Stephan when he called.

Four months later, on an impulse, Vera met Stephan for dinner. To her surprise, it turned out to be a delightful dinner.

After dinner, Stephan took her hand and said, "Thanks for joining me for dinner. I enjoyed it very much."

Stephan started walking away as Vera stood there thinking, *He seems to be very nice.*

Her thoughts were interrupted when Stephan turned around and said, "Oh, by the way, I have two theater tickets for tomorrow night to see the new play, 'Casanova.' I don't have anyone to go with me." He made a sad face. "So I was wondering if you would like to go with me. Oh, and by the way, I did not get the tickets because I want to be like Casanova," Stephan said, laughing out loud.

"I have heard this line before." Vera smiled.

"What makes you feel this is a line?" Stephan felt his face getting red, as he was taken aback by her bluntness.

"Your reputation..." Vera smirked. "In regard to the play, yes, that would be lovely," Vera replied, laughing.

Vera then started to go home, as it was close to the eight o'clock curfew set by Vladimir.

After that, Vera and Stephan began spending more and more time together. Vera was learning what Stephan's world was like.

XIV

As the events with the Communist Party were unfolding, Vladimir continued to be pessimistic about the future of his country.

Vladimir was not sure how to begin. All of a sudden, he started to talk.

"Since the Communist Party took over, things have been deteriorating rapidly. Let's face it, we are a Soviet-style state, and the Kremlin is going continue taking everything away from us. They don't care if we are suffering or if we don't have anything to eat. I think we would be better off if we would get out of here, before the Communist Party takes over everything."

"What?" Vera's mother asked, looking at him in surprise. "Do you mean escape from here?"

Vladimir nodded his head.

"Oh, my God! Are you crazy?" Vera's mother was in shock.

"I need a glass of vodka," Babushka said as she went for the vodka.

This was the first time Veruska saw her mother standing up for herself and father hesitating.

"Darling, listen to me, I can get a job as a doctor on one of the luxurious cruise ships. We would be able to go around the world. Once we find a country to which we would like to migrate, we would try settling there. Just imagine being able to have economic and social freedom."

"We would if we could, but we can't just pick up and leave." For the first time, Vera's mother was confronting Vladimir.

Vladimir ran his hand through his hair. "I have decided that I'm leaving with or without you."

"This is out of the question! We cannot just drop everything and leave," Babushka said as she took a sip of her vodka, walked toward the window, and looked outside. "My husband and this entire family have worked very hard to build this business and this big house. We devoted our entire lives to this land and to this country."

She turned and looked into Vladimir's eyes before telling him, "I will not walk away from all this. Our culture and history are here. This is crazy!"

"It doesn't have to be forever, we can return once Czechoslovakia is no longer under The Iron Curtain domain," Vladimir explained.

"Come back to what? This house and our business would be gone and we would have to start all over." Babushka took another sip of her vodka.

Vladimir looked at his wife, hoping she would change her mind and support him.

She was looking down as tears rolled down her face.

"Vladimir, how can we leave everything behind? We survived under the Nazi regime, we can survive under Communism."

Vladimir shook his head. He felt alone and defeated, knowing he could not fight the entire family.

He walked toward his wife and, with his hands, he lifted her face so she would look at him. "I can't bear the thought of leaving you and this family...I just can't do it on my own...so we are staying."

This was the only time Vladimir gave into the pressure of his family.

Babushka raised her glass and made a toast.

A few weeks later, the Communist Party started taking possession of everything. There were signs of military occupation everywhere, including trenches and walls made of coils of razor wire.

Buildings were ransacked, looted, abandoned, or just neglected. Why should anyone take care of a building he or she once owned when now it belonged to a corrupt government?

Vladimir's house was expropriated and divided four units.

The second floor was subdivided into two units, one unit rented to Vladimir and the other to an elderly woman.

The small room on the first floor became Babushka's apartment.

The entire third floor was transformed into a business unit, as was the first-floor space, which had been the storage space used for their moving company.

All tenants in the building shared the bathroom with the toilet.

The Communist Party censored everything, there was no free press, and people's mail was opened. The party even had the freedom to monitor phone conversations if they thought people were working against the party. Vladimir regretted not having moved the family away from all it.

Every day he would tell himself, *This cannot be happening to us, this is a nightmare, and there is no way of getting out.*

Every aspect of Vera's life turned bleak and black as the days went by. She could see pain in her parents' eyes as things continued to deteriorate around them.

One rainy afternoon, Vera and Stephan decided to go for a drink after they had been to a movie.

They were seated opposite each other sipping a beer when all of a sudden Vera had a smirk on her face.

"What's that smirk?" Stephan asked.

"Can you believe it has been six months since we met?"

"Aren't those the happiest six months of your life?" Stephan asked.

Vera laughed out loud.

"You know what? You are absolutely right. Every night before I go to sleep I say *Thank you, God, for putting*

Stephan in my life. I'm so fortunate."

"That's right and don't you forget it."

Vera grinned. "Wrong! It is more like this: *God, I must have done something really, really bad in my previous life. Please forgive me! I don't deserve such a harsh punishment."*

"You are so funny," Stephan said, laughing.

After that, there was a long silence between them.

"Darling, what are you thinking?" Vera asked.

"Do you remember what life was like before Communism?" Stephan was looking at Vera, his stare intense. "This is not life," he continued. "The Kremlin is destroying our culture, and has buried our heritage. Our living standard has fallen behind all other countries." He paused for a second. "There is no order, only chaos and corruption."

"Don't think I don't understand what you are feeling." Vera also felt the frustration with the situation.

"We are being treated like dirt. There are shortages of everything. How long did you stand in line to buy tooth-paste, toilette paper, and two bananas?" Stephan asked.

"Four hours." Vera was looking him straight in the face. "Four hours to get one small tube of toothpaste. I was only allowed to buy one at the time. I got one roll of toilet paper that feels like you are wiping your ass with sandpaper. And two bananas that in most countries would be considered spoiled and thrown in the garbage." Vera paused, locking eyes with him.

"To them we aren't people! We are shit!" Stephan was getting angry.

"The only people that have a good lifestyle are those working for the regime or people with a party connection," Vera said. "Our supposed-to-be Communist government has been transformed into a one-party state."

"The regime controls the media—look at the news and the articles—they are all Communist propaganda," said Stephan. "Despite enormous problems with corruption, poverty, and shortages of everything including food, the Communist government seems determined to project happy images worldwide."

Stephan pointed at the *Pravda* newspaper. "Did you see what is happening this week? 'We care about you and your health' is the heading of the article. The picture displays a certificate awarded by a team of human rights inspectors from Europe. The party is using this image as propaganda for the Russians. The party started a publicity campaign showing how they care for the workers' well-being. We all know what a lie this is; they show workers in factories with new ventilation systems pumping cool and clean air. They show how happy they are working under fluorescent lights and freshly painted walls. You and I know this is Communist propaganda and those are lies."

Stephan felt hopeless. "They display a falsified certificate from the human rights inspectors. In reality our factories are sweatshops...where women and children work in cruel conditions, dirty, without any ventilation or hygiene, and they are so underpaid."

Stephan was getting angry. "Take a look at this other story. Four people were shot and killed in a MacDonald's restaurant in the United States. It goes on telling us that this is why you don't want to live in a democratic country because people get killed every day. You don't think I know what is happening with this country?"

Vera could not prevent the tears from flowing down her face.

Stephan hesitated before he said, "I want to fight for an ideal...the ideal of freedom, not a land, not a president, and not a religion. I'm going to fight for our freedom." Stephan smiled.

"What do you mean you are going to fight for our freedom?" Vera asked.

"I have sworn to live free!" Stephan said firmly.

"Stephan, please do not do anything foolish. You should keep a low profile." Vera touched his hands.

Vera was horrified, wondering what Stephan had in mind.

XV

It began with a small group of men and women meeting in secret, creating an underground cell. Stephan, Olga, and Andrei were the leaders of the group.

Andrei was a very slim, middle-aged man, clean shaven with narrow eyes and dark hair, born and raised In Prague. He worked as an accountant for the government.

Olga was a stocky Russian woman, tall with black hair and bushy eyebrows. She was a teacher at Prague University.

"We will call ourselves *We Want Our **FREE**dom Revolution*," Stephan announced to the group.

The group applauded.

"We are fighting for freedom and against corruption," Olga yelled and raised her right fist up in the air.

The group cheered.

Everyone raised their right fist and started chanting.

"Together we are one force!"

"We are the force of freedom!"

"Together we are many!"

"No more corruption!"

"We want our freedom!"

There was another wave of applause, stomping, and howling.

They set up a clandestine printing press to produce anti-Communist pamphlets.

"We are printing anti-Communist pamphlets and posting them all over Prague. We want to spark a peaceful uprising," Olga said and smiled.

A few weeks went by and they realized the majority of the Czech people were not interested in politics because they had no faith changing the system.

"We have been making the people aware of our cause for weeks. Now it is time to move to the next phase. We must schedule a mass demonstration to show our force and tell the Communist Party we want fair treatment," Andrei said, proudly.

Stephan had decided not tell Vera much about his involvement with this group; he knew how dangerous it was. He couldn't believe how often he found himself thinking of her.

The first rally was scheduled a month later.

Stephan, Olga, and Andrei were making sure everything was ready for the rally. They had put together all the banners and signs and they had asked everyone to wear blue jeans, blue shirts, and blue caps.

The next morning the sky was clear and sunny. One hour prior to the rally, Stephan thought to himself, *Why is always a small number of people that are willing to take the risk to motivate the rest of the population?*

"Olga, in less than fifteen minutes the rally is scheduled to start, and we have only a few dozen supporters. This is not enough to make an impact. This is going to be a disaster." Stephan sounded worried and disappointed. "Is this going to be a total disaster?"

"Damn! Don't they understand they are not alone? We need to show that the majority of the Czech people are united and will not take this anymore."

"You are right!" Stephan hugged her before grabbing the megaphone. "It is always a small number of people who are willing to make the effort and to pay the high cost."

"Hello… hello… Can you hear me?"

The crowd cheered.

"Dear Czechoslovakians, comrades, bothers, and sisters, welcome!"

"Thank you for coming and supporting this rally from *We Want Our Freedom Revolution.*"

More applause and whistling.

"Today is a great day because for the first time the Czech people are here united as one. We are here to demonstrate to this government that we are ready to fight for our rights and justice."

"Our message today is a message of comradeship and solidarity."

The crowd started stomping and howling.

"I know many of you wanted to support our cause but were afraid of police retaliation. Let me reassure you that there isn't going to be any retaliation because this is a peaceful rally. The international press is here to document our peaceful rally so I urge you to support this rally. We, the Czech people, have an obligation to do everything in our power to help end the destabilization in this country. The only way to do this is if we all come together. This is not only for you but also for the generations to come." Stephan paused for a few seconds.

There was a wave of applause, stomping, and howling.

"Let me make it very clear we want this march to be peaceful. Our only weapons are banners and signs. We are asking for more freedom and the end of corruption. The Czech people need to stand up and let the party know that human rights violations and corruption are not acceptable to the people of this country."

"We, the Czech people, want to live together in peace and as equals, to bring freedom, peace, happiness, and prosperity to every person living in Czechoslovakia. Let us join hands as friends, brothers, and sisters to build a better life for all. We, the Czech people must work together to achieve a life without corruption…a life of peace. We cannot be silent. "

There was another wave of applause, stomping and howling from the audience. Stephan stood there facing them, overwhelmed by emotion.

All over the crowd, people waved banners.

Stephan paused and looked very slowly around the crowd. For a quick second it felt like the world had stopped. No wind, no movement, and no sound.

Stephan smiled and yelled, "Long live the freedom and dignity of the Czech people."

The crowd went crazy. Everyone could feel the power and intensity of the feeling generated by his words.

Stephan looked at Olga and Andrei before saying, "Let's start the rally."

The young and the old gathered. As they left the Strahov Stadium, and started to march down the street, the number of supporters started to increase. They flooded the main streets of Prague, marching over Malá Strana Square heading toward the center of Prague.

As they were approaching the center of Prague, the Red Army surrounded them. The protesters tried standing their ground in peace.

The world watched the standoff between the protestors and the Red Army, wondering if a civil war was going to erupt.

As the number of the armed guards surrounding them increased, so did the tension between the two groups.

Stephan, Olga, and Andrei knew the group wasn't large enough to stand their ground. They also sensed that they were in danger and decided to call off the demonstration.

With everyone wearing blue, it was easy for them to blend into the populace and get away from the soldiers.

A week after this incident the Communist Party was under fire from the European community to give in to some of the demands of the protestors.

The Communist Party decided to make a few promises to ease the international situation.

As time went by, Stephan realized that the new promises were a big farce.

"We are so stupid! It is obvious the party is trying to gain more time to capture and kill all of us," Stephan said angrily.

He was right. Moscow decided it was time to make them accountable for their action. They wanted the leaders of the resistance captured.

"More than half of our key people are in jail or in graves. According to the party, many of those in graves have 'committed suicide.' All of a sudden, suicide has become popular in Prague—the numbers have tripled."

"We need to act fast and continue fighting for our cause," Andrei told Stephan.

"Yes, you are right," Stephan answered. He knew they were running out of time.

That evening there were fire bombings and car bombings throughout the city of Prague.

The following day, there was mass demonstration that

paralyzed Prague. Protestors mobbed the street and chanted:

"Together we are one force!"

"We are the force of freedom!"

"Together we are many!"

"No more corruption!"

"We want our freedom!"

For the time being, the Communist Party had to abandon plans to crash the resistance, as pressure from the European community increased.

"Stephan, have you seen all the people at this demonstration? This is huge. I think it gives us hope that we might be heard and taken seriously this time," Andrei told him while they were marching with the protestors.

"Not so fast, we are still in a lot of danger," Stephan said nervously.

"What do you mean? They will not do anything right now, there are too many of us."

"They might not do anything right now but they just transferred Inspector Poděbrad from Moscow."

"Who is he?" Olga asked.

"Inspector Poděbrad is working with the secret police…Silovoki, the core of the Communist regime. This Silovoki group holds half the leadership positions in our ministries, agencies, and state-run companies. They are the new Communist Party working directly with the Kremlin."

"They received all the benefits and privileges of the party but the rules don't apply to them. They are very powerful."

"Inspector Poděbrad is a ruthless man who will stop at nothing to get what he wants. He supposedly uses the waterboarding tactic."

"Waterboarding tactic? What is that?" Andrei asked.

"It is when a prisoner is restrained and blindfolded while the interrogator pours water onto his face and into his mouth. It will make you feel like you are drowning."

"You see, it is all about perception. It is the same as if you hold a pistol to someone's head and fire a blank bullet. When you believe someone is going to kill you, you will say anything you think your captors want to hear, whether true or false, to save your life. The result is the same as using extreme violence."

"We have to be very careful. This man will be out to get us." Stephan's voice rose.

The demonstration lasted twenty-four hours. Stephan and his group asked to meet face-to-face with the Communist Party leaders. They also asked that international reporters to be present at the meeting to guarantee that they would not be walking into a trap. They demanded an answer within forty-eight hours; otherwise, another mass demonstration would take place.

XVI

Stephan and Vera went out for a nice romantic dinner. During dinner Stephan wondered if Vera would become angry if she learned of his involvement with the resistance group. He decided not to worry about it and enjoy the evening. He felt it would be too dangerous to tell Vera anything. He knew he was being watched all the time.

After dinner, they went for a walk in the old town. Stephan embraced Vera. She smiled at him, as she felt safe with his arms around her.

After their walk, they were seated on the rough bench right outside of Stephan's apartment. He had moved from Aunt Maci's.

Stephan took Vera's hand and said, "Do you want to come in?"

Vera nodded and gave him a warm and seductive smile as they entered the apartment.

He lived in a small—but very nice—part of a house that the party had divided into three units. His apartment consisted of a living room, a small bedroom, a very small bathroom, and a kitchenette. There wasn't much furniture, just the essentials: a small sofa, two chairs, a coffee table, and a nice rug spread across the hardwood floor.

Stephan looked into her eyes and wanted to touch and explore every inch of her body.

They embraced. Both of them could feel the heat and the passion between them.

Her lips touched his.

Vera grabbed the palm of his hands and pulled his arms back.

She kissed his right bicep, which had a black tattoo of two skulls.

"Now, let me give you a little bit of heaven...I'm going to be in control and you are not to do anything." She smiled.

Vera undid his tie and asked, "Do you trust me?"

"Yes...I think I do." Stephan laughed out loud. "What do you have in mind?" Stephan asked curiously.

"You will see." Vera smiled in a sinister way. "Don't move, just trust me." Vera gave him an evil laugh. She took the tie and blindfolded him.

She walked to the light switch and turned off the light. Then she reached out and extinguished one candle flame, leaving only one small candle lit.

Vera led Stephan to bed, and started to loosen his clothes.

Stephan's hands grabbed her as he tried feeling her sensual curves.

"Hey! What are you doing?" Vera asked, as she pulled

his arms back. "I told you, I'm in control now. I'm giving you pleasure. You are under my command so you cannot do anything, and that includes touching me."

"Sorry, I couldn't help it," Stephan said as passion started rising in him.

Vera removed his clothes.

She kissed him again.

She guided his body toward the bed, making him lay on his stomach, still blindfolded.

Vera took off her clothes and for a few minutes she stood by the bed staring at his naked body.

Stephan started to go crazy with anticipation.

He started to say, "Where are…"

"Quiet! No talking. I'm in control," Vera quickly interrupted him.

"I'm sorry!" Stephan murmured.

Vera waited a few more minutes.

She moved her body as close as she could to his without touching his naked body.

Both bodies were so close to each other that Stephan could feel the heat being generated from her body.

Stephan's body started to tremble with anticipation.

He moaned as Vera lips started kissing his bare back.

After awhile Vera stopped kissing him. Vera stood still, looking at him.

To Stephan's surprise, Vera said nothing.

Stephan could hear his heart racing as he was anticipating what was coming next.

Vera waited for a while, driving Stephan crazy.

Suddenly, Vera started to move quietly as Stephan tried anticipating what was happening next.

Stephan started to feel her silky hair slowly brushing against his legs and buttocks, and slowly going up toward his back.

Once her hair stopped touching his skin, her fingers started very gently caressing another part of his body.

"Oh, my God! You are driving me crazy." Stephan mumbled, as all that anticipation unleashed an incredible desire for passion.

Stephan's body was moving and begging her for more pleasure.

Vera turned him around and started to caress him slowly.

Stephan was on the verge of losing control. His moans were becoming louder.

His body was moving up and down, asking for more.

Vera's tongue gently started to lick his nipples. Her tongue could taste his salty skin.

Vera grabbed Stephan's hands as she sat on top of him.

Suddenly Vera squeezed Stephan's nipples so they would hurt just a little, pushing him to the edge of pain and pleasure.

She turned Stephan on his side and slapped his ass.

"What the hell..." Stephan said as his body jumped, surprised by her action.

Vera laughed and said, "You see! I'm not that innocent. I can do nasty also."

"You are a true Gemini," Stephan replied. "On one hand, you look to be very fragile, delicate, and innocent. On the other hand, you are a woman that knows exactly how to drive a man crazy with desire and passion," Stephan whispered.

Vera smirked.

"I cannot take it anymore. I beg you..." Stephan pleaded.

Vera turned her body, pulling Stephan in top of her.

Both bodies started to move as one, moving in the same rhythm.

Stephan could feel the sweat dripping from his forehead.

Both of them were moaning with desire. They could not contain it any longer.

A few minutes later, they were lying next to each other catching their breath.

Vera's face was lying on top of Stephan's chest. She shut her eyes for a while enjoying that nice feeling.

"You are amazing. Men must fall at your feet all the time," Stephan whispered as his arms wrapped around her.

Veruska

A few hours later, Stephan was sleeping. Vera moved slowly out of bed and dressed silently.

She needed to be back at her parents' house before daybreak.

Babushka had told Vladimir that Vera was feeling tired and she had gone to bed early so she needed to be back before they were up.

XVII

The following day the Red Army stopped a vehicle packed with explosives that blew up and instantly killed those inside.

The government declared a state of emergency for twenty-four hours. A curfew went into effect as a measure to stop further escalation of violence.

Everything deteriorated quickly. Authorities charged Stephan and his group with trying to create chaos and said they were responsible for the blown-up vehicle.

"We had nothing to do with the car full of explosives. This is just an excuse so Inspector Poděbrad to go after us." Stephan paused for a second. "The police have already arrested Olga for helping the anti-Soviet group." There was frustration in Stephan's voice.

Stephan was right. Inspector Poděbrad began moving quickly and aggressively, raiding many places and arresting many people.

Unfortunately, there wasn't enough time to put together another big rally.

Stephan and his group had to move and go into hiding. They felt that they were about to be crushed by the regime.

They did not realize that it was the beginning of a revolution. There was a growing agreement among the people that more had to be done to stop all the corruption and violence.

Four days had passed since the government had declared a state of emergency and Vera had lost touch with Stephan.

She reached for the phone and dialed Eva's number.

"Hello, Eva, dear, how are you? Have you heard from or seen Stephan?" Vera could feel her voice trembling.

"No, the last time we talked was four nights ago. He is probably busy studying for his final exams."

"I know he is probably fine." Vera was frustrated. "I just worry because I have read in the newspapers that they raided many places, some were set on fire, and many people have been arrested. I know I worry too much." Vera laughed. "Oh, yes, I'm fine."

"I know things could be much worse."

"Yes, I will see you this afternoon."

"Bye."

Vera put the receiver down.

He is coming today to see me, she kept telling herself, as she was sitting in the living room gazing into the bright fire, wondering where and why Stephan had vanished.

Later that day, Vera walked downstairs to get the mail. To her surprise there was a letter addressed to her in Stephan's handwriting.

She took it upstairs, opened it, and started reading.

The letter read:

Dear Veruska:

By now, you are probably worried and wondering where I disappeared to.

By the time you read this letter I will be far away, hopefully in another country.

I know this is very hard to believe but, trust me, what I am doing is for the good of both of us.

The time we spent together has been the happiest time of my life. You are a very special person and this was a very hard decision for me.

Given what has happened lately, I decided it is best that we go our separate ways.

Right now, it is impossible for our relationship to work out. We probably will never see each other again.

Just remember one very important thing...I love you. I will never forget you and the wonderful time we had together.

Please don't hate me too much. I am out of your life. Please don't make any attempt to find me.

I love you.

Stephan

Trembling like a leaf, she read the letter repeatedly, hoping to convince herself that she was not the victim of a horrible nightmare. She wondered what went wrong. She was in tears.

Vera did not hear Babushka come in; she was too engrossed in the letter.

"What's wrong, Veruska?"

"It is a letter from Stephan. He is saying good-bye. He has left Prague."

She shook her head in disbelief and collapsed into Babushka's arms, sobbing.

"I know things look bad but he still might come back," Babushka said after Vera handed her the letter and she read it.

"No, he won't. Why should he? He is on this way going to a free country, why would be come back here?" Vera asked.

"You never know, my darling!" Babushka pressed her hand to Vera's head, trying to calm her down.

"Here is something to calm you down," Babushka told Vera as she handed her a small glass of orange juice. "I saw you bring in a letter earlier and by the look on your face, I had a feeling it might be bad news so I brought this with me to help make you feel better."

Vera took a big sip of it started to cough. "Babushka this is so strong, what is this?"

"This is our 'family special calming remedy' that has

been in our family for many generations. It is guaranteed to make you forget all your troubles."

Vera tried taking another sip.

"This is way too strong for me," she said, as she put the glass down.

"One thing I learned from life is that things rarely come out as we planned," Babushka told Vera as she put her arm around her.

"Are you going to finish drinking this?" Babushka looked at the glass she had brought Vera.

"No, I'm not drinking that! It tastes awful! It tastes like vodka!" Vera replied.

"Darling, don't worry, I'll drink it," Babushka said as she picked up the glass and finished it.

"By the way, this was premium vodka." Babushka smiled.

"Could I have been so mistaken about him? I thought he loved me. It is obvious he didn't love me; he just took off."

"Veruska, don't jump to any conclusions. There could be other reasons for his actions." Babushka held her hand.

"You think so?"

"Just remember, things always happen for a reason. Have faith."

"Babushka, I love you so much. You always know what to say and I also love you for the *special remedy*."

Both of them were laughing uncontrollably.

XVIII

The following week, Babushka walked into Vera's room and said,

"Guess what I have here?"

"What?" Vera asked.

"A letter from Harold," she smiled.

"Give it to me! Let me see it!" Vera couldn't wait to read it.

Dear Veruska:

Darling, how are you?

This is a very quick note just to let you know I have been thinking of you. I miss you.

I am here in Sao Paulo, Brazil on a business trip working for the Foreign Department. I will be here for another three weeks.

I hope everything is going well with you and your family. I have been reading about all the demonstrations and police arrests in Prague and I'm so worried about you and your family safety.

I miss you so much. I keep imagining the day that I will be able to hold you in my arms again. I want to feel and touch you again and this time I will not let you go.

It seems like strange things are always happening to my family.

Veruska

Last week one of my cousins received a container from a relative of mine in Italy. They assumed it was some special type of special Italian spices.

That evening they decided to make a nice pizza for the entire family and they decide to try the new Italian spices.

According to them, it was the best pizza they ever had. Well, the following day they received a telegram from Italy informing them that they would receive some ashes from one of their friends. This friend's dying wish was to have his ashes strewn on Ipanema Beach. This friend had spent some time in Rio de Janeiro and that was the happiest time of his life.

My family decided they will never be able to eat that type of pizza again.

My mother is fine and getting used living by herself. I haven't talked to my father and I'm not sure what is happening with him.

I love you and I miss you very much. I still feel your touch and kisses in my dreams.

Please write to me soon and take care of yourself.

Big Kisses.

I Love you.

Harold

XIX

Five months had passed since Stephan left. Vera was trying to move on with her life. Her life became dull, a tedious routine.

Vera, like everybody else, was having a hard time adjusting to the new lifestyle since Czechoslovakia became part of the Iron Curtain.

The five-pointed Red Star, the official symbol of Communism, representing the five fingers of the worker's hand, could be found everywhere.

Wherever you looked, you could see neglected or abandoned buildings.

Corruption was widespread.

People never smiled, they were unhappy.

All the good Czech merchandise that existed was imported to Moscow.

Fashion was dictated by what was available in the stores, and there were few styles available. The colors selection generally consisted of either brown or black. You were not allowed to try anything on and nothing was returnable.

There were only three TV stations; one broadcast from Moscow, the second aired only Communism propaganda, and the third broadcast only limited news censored by the party plus a few Russian movies.

People struggled to survive—they looked so miserable.

There was shortage of everything. One had to stand in line for hours to get a few items and they were the lowest quality.

"Darling, we are going to need sharper steak knives to cut this meat." Vladimir smiled at Vera's mother who tried smiling. She waited in line at the store for hours and was allowed to buy a few pieces of meat and two bananas.

"I'm so sorry. Can you believe I stood in line for three hours so I could buy this piece of meat and the two bananas?"

"The meat is too tough on my dentures. I cannot eat it. I will have another glass of vodka instead," Babushka announced.

"Have you seen the two bananas? They are so brown and soft you must eat them today."

"Mother, why did you spend so much time buying this?"

"Well, I wanted to make us a nice dinner." Vera's mother took a deep breath. "Plus I know how much you like bananas."

"Mother, you know that since the Russians took over, there is nothing worth buying and this was probably very expensive."

"I know there is nothing worth buying in this country," Vera's mother sadly admitted.

Vladimir smiled and replied, "You see, my dear, I'm not as dumb as you may think when it comes to investment. I made the right decision when I invested our money in gold, paintings, and diamonds. They don't lose their value and the Communist pigs will not take them away from us."

"Yes, we already knew that," said Vera.

"Let's make a toast to Vladimir!" Babushka raised her glass of vodka.

"To Vladimir!" They all toasted and started to laugh.

"Mother, thanks for dinner. It was delicious. May I be excused? I'll be right back." Vera had decided to go outside and get some fresh air in the backyard.

It was a nice evening, the summer rainstorm had passed, the sky was clear.

Vera was staring at the stars and thinking about Stephan *Where is he? Did he really escape? Is he happy?*

Suddenly her thoughts were interrupted as she heard a noise coming from the shadows in the garden.

Strangely, she wasn't frightened.

"Who is there?" she asked.

"Hello, Vera," came a voice from behind the bushes. Vera froze for a second as she recognized the voice.

"It's me, Stephan," he whispered carefully.

"Where are you?"

She could hear footsteps coming from the bushes behind her.

She turned around slowly as Stephan stepped into the clearing.

Vera stared at him in a harsh way. She was silent, not knowing what to say.

Stephan smiled at her. He put his gun in the back pocket of his pants and walked toward her. He was staring into her eyes. Her eyes were cold. The moment he saw her he wanted very badly to kiss and hold her. He touched her bare arms instead. Her skin was so soft. He missed touching her.

Vera tried gathering her thoughts, but she wasn't sure what to think. She was skeptical. She could feel her anger rising inside of her.

Stephan grabbed her and kissed her, but she showed no emotion.

She tried to look steadily at Stephan, but her eyes moved. She was looking toward the back door of her parents' house.

"How did you get into the backyard without my parents seeing you?"' Vera asked.

"The gate was…"

"Sh-h-h—did you hear something?"

She was looking around. "Don't make a sound," she said, nervously.

"Let me take a look around… hold on." Vera walked toward the house to see if someone was there.

Vera came back a moment later.

"Stephan? Are you still here?"

"Yes, I'm here…I must see you," he pleaded. "Please meet me here at midnight."

She grabbed his hands, which were very cold. She realized

how much she missed him.

"Why should I? I must be crazy because I'm still talking to you. One day you just decided to disappear. You wrote me a letter telling me that you were leaving. No other explanation!" She paused for a second. "You decided! It was all about you. I was not that important to have any say in your decision, was I?"

Stephan could see the hurt in her eyes.

"A few days after you took off, the police came looking for you. They told me you were one of the top leaders of the resistance group. I had no idea that you were so involved."

"Listen to me. For your own safety, you don't know where I am and you don't know anything," Stephan pleaded with her.

"We don't have to worry about that because I don't know anything about your life anyway. Do I?" Vera asked, sarcastically.

"You could have been dead for all I knew. Now, out of the blue, you appear again in the middle of the night. Tell me one thing...do you expect me to pretend that nothing has happened?" Vera's frustration was coming out. "I really don't care to see you anymore."

"I know you have all the right to be angry with me...But please give me ten minutes to explain." He paused. "After that, if you still don't want to see me I will take off and I promise you...You will never see me again."

"Veruska!" Vladimir was calling her.

"Sh-h-h, my father is calling."

"Veruska, please meet me later. I have come back to Prague because of you. I have risked my life to see you."

Gradually Vera's cold expression started changing and the old look was coming back as she said, "Yes! Yes! Very well, I'll be here." She was looking toward the house.

"Now please go before my father sees you!"

As she turned around and started walking toward the house, she could see her father coming out of the house.

"Veruska, where are you?" Vladimir called again.

Vera waited for a moment and slowly walked toward her father.

"There you are," Vladimir said. "Hurry inside, we are having dessert and Babushka wants another glass of vodka."

Both started laughing as they went inside.

Right at midnight, Vera climbed out the first-floor window as quietly as possible, and waited patiently for Stephan. She started to think how much she had missed him.

Fifteen minutes later Stephan appeared.

"Veruska, my darling! Thank you for agreeing to meet me and letting me explain everything. By the way, you look more beautiful than the last time I saw you." Stephan was staring at her.

"Ohhh no! Don't you start using flattery to get out of this." Vera laughed. Deep inside she was happy seeing him.

"You have all the right to hate me. Let me start by telling you that I'm crazy about you."

Vera wanted to kiss him but did not dare show any affection toward him, until she heard his explanation.

"Don't you realize I have risked my life to come back to Prague? The only reason I came back was to see you be-cause...because I love you and cannot live without you. I had to leave Prague. That night after we had dinner I almost got killed."

"Killed?" Vera was stunned. "What? Why didn't you tell me?"

"I didn't want to put your life in danger. That was why I didn't tell you about my deep involvement with the resistance group. I was trying to protect you. Actually, the fact that I'm back here doesn't change anything, I am putting both of our lives in danger. It all started after we had dinner. Inspector Poděbrad and his men stopped a car full of explosives, the car blew up...You remember that...don't you?" Stephan was looking at Vera.

"Yes, I do! It was all over the news." Vera remembered it because that story was the beginning of a government PR campaign describing to the Czech people how Inspector Poděbrad was bringing peace to Prague by destroying the anti-Soviet groups.

"The regime condemned any group that complained about the present situation in this country. They claimed they had found a link between us and the attempted car bombing." Stephan paused.

"Inspector Poděbrad used that incident as an excuse and start raiding many places and arresting many of us. We were also accused of killing two soldiers." Stephan took a deep breath. "Our Olga was one of the first people to get arrested that day."

"Oh! Poor Olga. Is she OK?" Vera asked.

"We...We don't know." Stephan stared into the distance.

"What do you mean, you don't know? Do you mean she is still in jail? Poor Olga. We must get her out of there. I can ask my father..."

"No, she supposedly was released from jail. She has vanished. No one has seen her since then."

"Where did she go? We should try contacting her family." Her eyes were teary because she knew what the answer was.

"We already contacted her parents and her sister and they haven't heard from her."

Stephan grabbed Vera's hand and looked into her eyes.

"We think they killed her."

"Noooo! That cannot be true." Vera shook her head in horror.

Stephan reached out to touch her.

Vera started sobbing.

"I knew right away that the only way for me to survive was to go into hiding," Stephan said as he caressed Vera's hair. "I knew Inspector Poděbrad would stop at nothing until he captured me. There was no time to let you know what was happening. I went to my apartment, packed a small bag, and went to Andrei's apartment." Stephan paused.

"Everything was falling apart and evolving into a huge mess. That evening Inspector Poděbrad came to Andrei's apartment looking for us. He wanted to take us back to the police headquarters. Andrei and I locked ourselves in Andrei's apartment building." Stephan tried smiling at Vera.

"We heard him tell another policeman, and I quote, 'Yes, do anything necessary to capture them, even if it means killing them. Just don't let them escape.' Five minutes later, the building was on fire. We couldn't see anything. The apartment was filled with smoke. Andrei and I panicked and we were separated attempting to escape."

"This is so horrible, my poor darling," Vera said as she rested her head on his shoulder.

"Thick smoke was everywhere and I started choking and coughing. I tried holding my breath, but it was impossible. I started coughing again." Stephan paused.

"I remember looking at the building's entrance, it was engulfed in flames. I crawled on the floor and was very lucky to find a few broken floorboards. I managed to go under the floorboards, and I crawled all the way to the side of the building. I couldn't go anywhere because the police had surrounded the building." He took a deep breath.

Vera was looking at Stephan in disbelief.

"I was only able to get out when one of the policemen in front of the building started screaming, 'Stop or I'll shoot! Stop!' All the other policemen ran toward the front at the building." Stephan stopped for a second again, consumed by his emotions.

"This is so horrible, I cannot believe they got away with this." Vera was horrified.

"The only reason why I'm alive today is because of Andrei. After we got separated, he managed to get to the front of the building. He broke one of the front windows, got out into the street, and started to run away. He was chased by the policemen and gunned down on the street."

"Nooooo!" Vera shook her head and started crying again. She fell like she was going to faint.

"They murdered him. He was shot six times in the back. I know for sure he was carrying no guns. They simply shot a man in the back."

Stephan put his arms around Vera, looked straight into her eyes, and said, "Now do you understand why I had to disappear? I tried leaving you. I tried making you hate me. Unfortunately, I couldn't get you out of my mind. From the first moment I saw you I wanted you. When I wake up, I think of you. When I breathe, I think of you. When I sleep, I dream of you. I need you so much, I need your love," he whispered.

'Last week I knew I couldn't go on without you so I made up my mind to come back. Nothing else matters to me, only you."

Vera smiled at him.

"Even if I were killed trying, it would be worthwhile just to see you," Stephan said.

"When I reached the train station I knew it would be impossible for me to simply board the train to Prague. I managed, without anyone seeing me, to hide under the station platform. I waited until the train started to move and I was able to run and get under the train. It took all my strengths to be able to hold onto the undercarriage where I rode all the way to Kladno." He was smiling looking into Vera's eyes.

"My poor darling! Please forgive me for doubting you." Vera kissed him passionately.

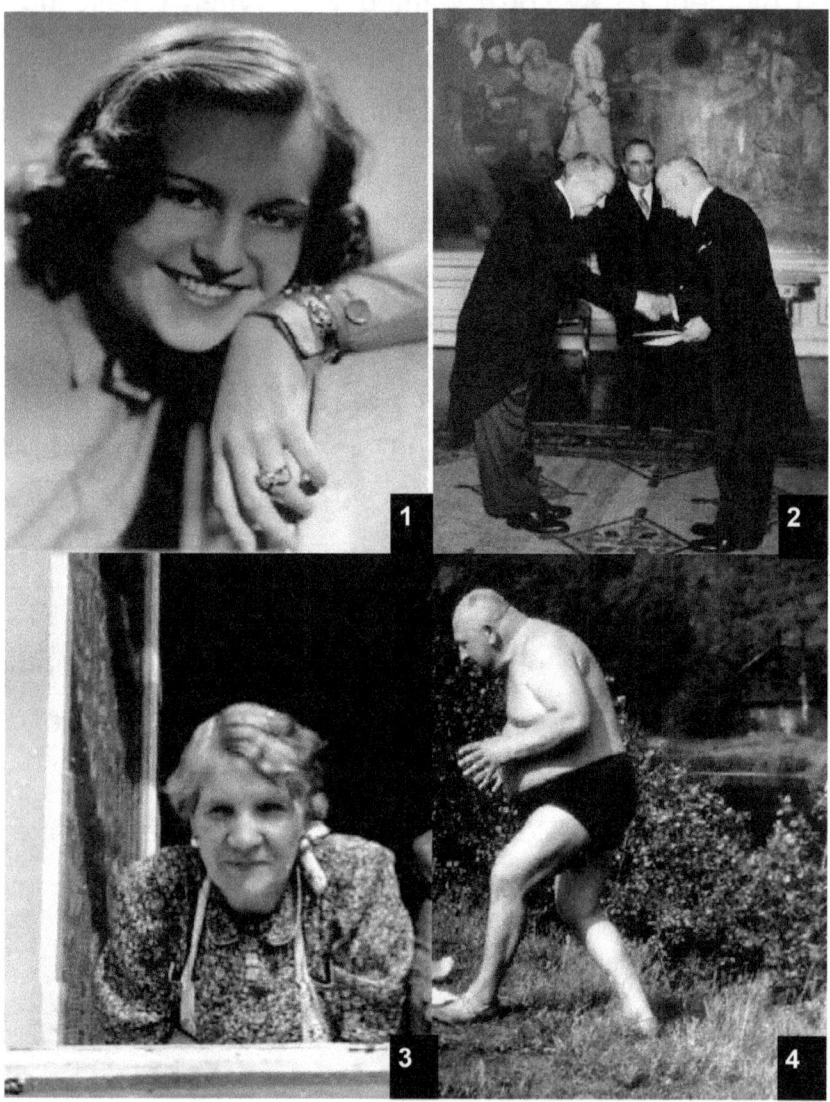

1) Veruska after she returned from boarding school in England.
2) Ambassador Coimbra greeting Edvard Beneš, the President of Czechoslovakia.
3) Babushka, Veruska's grandmother.
4) Inspector Poděbrad working for Silovoki, the secret police, was transferred from Moscow to capture Stephan and Veruska.

5) Veruska and her mother in Karlovy Vary.
6) Operation Anthropoid, Heydrich's car at the scene of his assassination.
7) Ambassador Martin, in Brazil, meeting with the Brazilian President Getulio Vargas.
8) Devín Castle/Danube River - The ruins stand on the frontier between Czechoslovakia (presently part of Slovakia) and Austria. That is where the Danube River is the narrowest and someone can try escaping into Austria.
9) SS Obergruppenführer Reinhard Heydrich.

1) Ambassador Martin Coimbra, left, arriving to the Prague Castle for a meeting with Edvard Beneš.
2) *Pražský hrad,* Prague Castle, one of the biggest castles in the world.

3) Foreign Minister Jan Masaryk ,left, meeting with Ambassador
Martin Coimbra and President Beneš.
4) Harold's mother, first woman right, with President Juan Peron of
Argentina.
5) Vladimir, Veruska's domineering father, head surgeon in a hospital near Prague.
6) Harold after he moved to Rome.
7) Veruska walking around Salzburg.

.

XX

.

Led by an anonymous tip, Inspector Poděbrad learned that Stephan was back in Prague.

This time, he will not escape. I will do everything in my power to capture him, he thought to himself. He was becoming obsessed with the idea of capturing Stephan.

Stephan and Vera were very careful not to raise any suspicions. They were extremely cautious, choosing where to meet, making sure that they were not being watched by an undercover policeman.

One late rainy afternoon, Vera and Stephan agreed to meet at a little out-of-the-way tavern in the old part of Prague. It was next to the Hotel Vladislav, behind the Malostranská Bridge tower.

Local neighborhood people frequented this small old tavern. Vera and Stephan felt safer there.

Vera walked in the tavern, which was very dark due to the low lighting, and very crowded, smoky, and noisy. She was wearing a black rayon dress clinging provocative to her curves, white gloves, and a white hat.

She was able to get a small table right away and ordered a Budějovický Budvar beer.

Five minutes later, Stephan walked into the tavern.

Before sitting, he walked around the tavern, checking to see if it was safe.

He ordered a beer and then walked very slowly toward Vera and asked, "Excuse me, but where have I seen you before?"

"Perhaps you have seen me at the university campus? You do go to the university?" Vera smiled at him.

"Yes."

"You probably have seen me there."

"You are probably right. Mind if I sit down?" Stephan asked.

"No, please go ahead," Vera said softly.

Once both of them thought it was safe and no one was listening to their conversation, Vera asked, "How are you, darling?"

"I'm fine, just getting tired of having to look over my shoulder everywhere I go."

Vera tried smiling but was feeling helpless.

"You know I cannot stay in hiding forever." Stephan was looking straight at her.

"Are you happy living here?" Stephan's eyes were fixed on Vera.

"No." She looked so sad.

"Are you satisfied living the rest of your life under these conditions?"

Shaking her head, Vera replied, "No."

She wanted to conceal her feelings, and forced a smile, shifting her focus away from her emotions.

"The reason why I'm asking you these questions is because you know I cannot continue living like this. This time I want us to decide our future together. As far as I know we have only two options."

Vera had a puzzled look on her face.

"We can live like this until I am caught...or I can escape again...I mean we can escape together."

"Escape?" Her voice was shaky.

"Yes, I can make arrangements for us to escape. I have some connections..."

Suddenly Stephan stopped as he looked toward the tavern entrance where a policeman had just walked in.

"We must get out of here," he whispered, as he sensed they were in danger.

The policeman was watching them intently, making them very uneasy.

Vera and Stephan looked at each other and they decided to stop talking. They turned away from each other, pretending not to know each other.

Vera could feel the policeman's eyes staring at them.

Shortly, the policeman approached their table and asked to see Stephan's identification.

Stephan gave him a library card, his cousin's library card.

"Mr. George Novotni?" The policeman took at look at the card again. "So your name is George Novotni?"

"That's right." Stephan tried smiling.

"You know this is not a valid identification card? I need a driver's license or passport, something with your picture."

"I don't have my driver's license with me. It is back in my apartment but I promise you I will carry it with me all the time."

Stephan got up "I was actually leaving to go back to class."

"Not so fast! I'm afraid I cannot let you leave. I must take you down to the Barolomejska police station."

"Listen, Officer, I'm sorry I don't have my driver's license with me but I need to go to class. Please give me a break this time," Stephan pleaded with him.

"Mr. Novotni, please come with me."

"But why?" Stephan was trying to stay calm.

"You fit the description of someone wanted by Inspector *Poděbrad*."

"This is ridiculous! You cannot arrest me just because I don't have my identification. I gave you my library card. Plus I haven't done anything wrong."

"Sorry, I must take you in," The policeman told him.

"Please, I need to go to class."

"Come, let's go," the policeman insisted.

"I need to go to class, please get out of my way," Stephan said angrily.

He tried walking toward the tavern door.

"Don't do that!" commanded the policeman sharply. "I've told you not to do that."

"What do you mean?" Stephan raised his voice.

"You are going nowhere except to the police station with me."

"You cannot take me." Stephan shouted.

"Oh yes, I can," said the policeman, putting a hand on Stephan's chest to stop him from leaving.

"I'm warning you, back away from me." Stephan's stare was intense and hostile. He was beside himself.

"You are not very friendly. What are you attempting to accomplish? Do you know?" Stephan forced his way, pushing Vera aside, hoping she would leave.

"Oooh, and what will you do?" the policeman said as he shoved Stephan against the wall, throwing him off balance.

Stephan suddenly realized he was pinned against the wall, unable to defend himself.

The policeman's hands were on Stephan's throat.

Stephan found some strength to push him away from him.

Suddenly, he heard Vera screaming "Stephan! Watch out!"

In the corner of his eye, he saw a fist swinging toward his face. The fist hit his face, causing him to step back so he wouldn't fall down.

Stephan was caught off guard. He felt an immediate pain on the right side of his face. He had slumped against the wall unable to avoid the other fist about to hit his stomach. Stephan let out a moan, when the fist hit his stomach.

"Do not move, stand still," the policeman commanded as he drew a pistol from his coat.

Vera was standing in the crowd. She could not breathe. She didn't know what to do.

"Wait!" Stephan held up his hands in defiance.

"You are lying," the policeman said, pointing the gun at Stephan. "You are coming with me now."

Stephan said nothing, his eyes growing colder and full of rage.

He turned around and started walking away from the policeman.

"Stop or I'll shoot! Stop him!" shouted the policeman as he put his finger on the trigger.

"Nooooh!" Vera screamed as she grabbed a bottle of wine from the table and started swinging it toward the policeman.

The next second she could feel her hand getting wet when the bottle of wine shattered against the policeman's head.

Blood started to flow, covering part of the policeman's face. His gun was still pointed at Stephan.

Stephan struck the policeman with both hands, grabbed him, and his right fist pounded the policeman's stomach, knocking him back out of their path. He hit the policeman again and he dropped the gun on the floor.

"Stephan, stop it!" Vera pleaded with him.

Stephan stood still. He was staring at Vera and then

he whispered in her ear. "Go on, Vera! Run! Go home. I'll get in touch with you. If you get caught now we will never be able to realize our plans. Go now!"

"Yes, Yes," she murmured. "All right, I'll go in a moment." Her hands, lips, and body were trembling.

"No, Vera, go now!" he screamed angrily.

Stephan looked at her. "Sorry, darling! Please go now. I'll get in touch with you I promise. Please go...run!" he said, apologetically with a tone of urgency.

"I love you!" Those were Stephan's last words to her before she turned and left.

Vera rushed up the steps out of the tavern. She started running home, not looking back. She spent a few minutes walking the streets close to her house. She was t
past her curfew hour.

"I'm so sorry I'm..." she started telling her father when she walked into the living room.

"You are late." Vladimir wasn't listening to her.

"Yes," Vera replied, "later than I intended." Her heart was pounding.

"What's the matter?" Vladimir inquired, looking at her suspiciously.

"What do you mean?" She took a deep breath, trying to stay calm.

"You look agitated and nervous...jittery."

"I have a bad headache and I think it is ridiculous that I have this curfew. I'm not a little girl, you know."

Vladimir was surprised with her rebellious tone of voice.

"You are under my roof and if you want to stay here, you will obey my rules. Do you understand me?" he asked her angrily.

"Loud and clear." Vera resented her father for controlling every aspect of her life.

Vera announced she was going to retire to her room, and did not come down again that evening.

Vera was trying to force herself to stay calm. She wasn't sure if Stephan was able to get out of the tavern safely. Everything had happened so quickly.

She started to think about Stephan's proposal of escaping together. She laid in bed thinking about her life. Deep inside she knew she should escape; otherwise, she would regret it and she would turn into one of those bitter, unhappy women.

XXI

It was early morning when Vera opened the front door and there stood a very short man with a small clipped mustache and small intense eyes behind round glasses.

"Miss Vera Pisova?" He asked.

"Yes," she replied.

"I'm awfully sorry to disturb you, I'm inspector Wladislav Poděbrad. I'm working with the Prague Police Department."

Vera froze for a second.

"May I come in? I would like to ask you a few questions about Stephan Lucas."

"Sure, come in, Inspector Pupubrad, but I can already tell you I don't know where Stephan is." Vera's voice was cold.

"Inspector Poděbrad," he said.

"What?"

"My name, my name is Inspector Poděbrad," he said patiently.

"Correct." Vera nodded.

"Do you know the whereabouts of Mr. Stephan Lucas?"

"I already told you. No, I don't. I don't know where he is." She nodded.

"Are you sure?" He hesitated for a second. "You have

been seen with him."

"Inspector Pupubrad," Vera said, as she stared at him dumbfounded. *How did he know I had met him?* she asked herself. "I ran into him but I don't where he is."

"My name is Inspector Poděbrad not Pupubrad."

"Yes, you already told me your name." Vera said rather sarcastically.

Inspector Poděbrad looked at her suspiciously. "I do not think you are telling me the truth. Are you?"

Vera didn't even dignify the question with an answer.

"I have no way of proving this, but I think you know where he is."

"Inspector Pupubrad, it gives me no pleasure to tell you what you must already know. He left..."

"Inspector Poděbrad," he tried correcting her.

"He left Prague months ago, at that time we were dating. One day he decided to leave without letting me know why or where he was going." Vera stopped to take a breath. She was choosing her words with caution. "Then one day, Stephan reappeared. I ran into him and our conversation was quite superficial."

"Did Stephan tell you why he came back? What he was planning to do? Or perhaps he told you where he was staying?"

She shook her head "No! No! and No! I have no idea. After the way he treated me, do you think I want to know what is happening with him?"

"You know he is wanted by the police. We just want to ask him some questions about his involvement with a car explosion that occurred some time ago."

"Inspector Pupubrad, one thing I know—because we were together when that happened—is that the charges against Stephan are absolutely ill founded and totally untrue."

"Poděbrad."

"I beg your pardon?" Vera gave him a warm smile.

"My name is pronounced Poděbrad." He rolled his eyes. "Well, that is what we are trying to determine. We just want to talk to him so we can clear this up. If you hear from Stephan, the smartest thing for you to do is to contact us right away."

With that the phone rang. *Thank God! Now he has to stop asking so many questions, I wish this interrogation would be over,* Vera was thinking to herself as she reached for the phone.

"Veruska, this is Eva. I'm so glad you answered the phone. Stephan wants to see you. He doesn't want to go over there because the police are looking for him and they probably will come and ask you some questions."

Vera was trying to stay calm. She held the receiver very close to her ear. "No I don't have your sweater..."

"What sweater? I'm talking about Stephan," Eva replied.

"No!" Vera's voice was shaky. "No, dear! As I said, I don't know where your sweater might be."

"What are you..." Eva started to say again.

"I will look for your sweater and I will call you back,"
Vera quickly interrupted Eva. "Inspector Pupubrad is here
so I must go. I will call you back shortly."

Vera smiled at the inspector, pretending everything
was fine.

"Oh no! the policemen are already there!" Eva whispered. "Now I understand why you were talking about the
sweater. Stephan wants to meet you at the department
store this afternoon at three."

"That's fine, Eva!" Vera smiled at the inspector. "I'll talk
to you then...Good-bye, Eva." She hung up the phone and
walked toward the inspector.

"That was my best friend, Eva."

"As I was saying before, the smartest thing for you to
do, if you hear from Stephan, is to contact us right away
and tell us where we can find him,." the inspector told her
impatiently. "You don't want to get involved with him again."
His voice was very entreating.

"But of course we will do that!" Vladimir said, emerging
from the other room. "We will always cooperate with the police."

"Mr. Pisova, how nice to meet you." Inspector Poděbrad
smiled at him.

Vladimir nodded. "Is that all, Inspector... ?"

"Inspector Pupu..." Vera's lips started to shake, as she
was in the verge of falling apart. Her knees buckled slightly.

"Inspector Wladislav Poděbrad," he interrupted Vera,

as he was determined to let Vladimir know his correct name.

Vladimir checked his watch. "Oh yes, Inspector Poděbrad, I don't want to be rude but we really are running late. Vera is going to the hospital with me."

Confused, Vera stood frozen for a moment until she realized her father was lying so they would get rid of the inspector.

"Oh, I'm so sorry to put you through all this questions. I won't take up any more of your time. I also must get back to the police station," he said as he started to walk toward the front door.

"Well, we will talk again," Vladimir responded, smiling at the inspector.

"If you remember something or have any other information that might be helpful, I would appreciate your calling me." He pulled his business card out of his pocket and handed it to Vera.

"Stephan is not exactly the man you believed him to be. He has led a strange dual existence. So please be careful, he can be a very dangerous man," the inspector warned Vera.

"This is my private phone number so you can reach me anytime day or night."

With his card in her hand, Vera insisted, "I'm telling you, I know nothing."

Inspector Poděbrad glanced at Vladimir and gave him a smile.

Vera's legs were trembling.

Vladimir waited until he heard the inspector's car drive down the street, and then he turned and looked at Vera.

He looked distressed. "Veruska, don't tell me you have something to do with all this?"

Vera shook her head. "No, Father, I don't know anything about this. I have seen Stephan a few times since he returned but I don't know what he is up to."

"Good! I just don't want anything to happen to you." Vladimir's voice was that of a concerned father. "You know I'm just trying to protect you." He gave her a loving smile.

Meanwhile, in the car, Inspector Poděbrad was telling himself as he drove off, *I know she knows more than she told me. The bitch wants to play games with me? She will be sorry. I don't care who her father is. Perhaps the doctor is also in it.*

XXII

It was 3:00 p.m., and Vera and Stephan were to meet in the department store in Prague.

Vera came up the stairs.

Stephan was staring at her, smiling—she looked so beautiful.

She was wearing a silk cashmere windowpane-plaid pencil skirt with a nice pair of snakeskin high heels that flattered her legs.

"Stephan, my darling, are you all right?

He smiled and said, "Yes, that was a very close call. Thanks for helping me with the policeman…"

Vera hugged him.

"Now you see? It is impossible for me to stay here. I cannot live like a prisoner, hiding the rest of my life. I'm putting you and me in danger. Darling, listen to me!" Stephan whispered, looking around to make sure no one could hear their conversation. "Everything is planned."

"What do you mean?" Vera asked.

"I have arranged with Judge Milosh for us to escape. I'm asking you to come with me." He smiled at her.

Vera took a deep breath and tried smiling back at him.

"Don't you want to come with me? Don't you want to

have a better life?" he asked her.

"Yeah, Yes." Vera looked into his eyes. "Yes, I want to go and I want to be with you." Vera's voice was shaky.

Stephan looked around again, making sure no one was near enough to listen to their conversation.

"This would mean leaving everything behind."

Vera nodded. She was scared.

"I want you, please, to make me a promise, namely, that you will say nothing to a single soul of what I'm about to tell you. You cannot tell anyone of our plans. Not even your family or your closest friends. Secrecy is the essence of our success."

He stopped and gave Vera a quick kiss. He grabbed her hands, trying to give her some reassurance that everything would work out fine.

"We will take the train to Kuty in Slovakia. Once we get to Kuty, Judge Milosh has arranged for a 'guide' to take us across the border into Austria. Once in Austria, we will get falsified Austrian passports." He paused for a second. "That will enable to cross through the Russian Zone."

Vera was listening carefully and her face showed how frightened she really was.

"I know this is not going to be easy for you, leaving your parents behind."

"Everything sounds so unreal," said Vera. "I always assumed Czechoslovakia would forever be my home." Vera was tearful.

XXIII

Right after dinner Vera pretended to be exhausted and told her parents she was going to bed early because she was going to the university about 6:00 a.m.

If everything went according to their plan, this was the last time she would seen them.

When she went to give her father a good night kiss she looked right into his eyes and she got a strange feeling that he knew what was happening.

For a split second, Vera contemplated telling her father about her plans but stopped herself.

She was doing everything possible not to show her real feelings and emotions.

She picked up the bottle of vodka, walked behind Babushka, and filled her glass before giving her a kiss.

Babushka was silent, just staring at her, wondering what was happening.

Vera gave her mother a very long hug. She didn't want to let her go.

As she walked up the stairs, she looked around the house trying to memorize ever single detail. She couldn't believe this was her last night at her parent's house.

In her room and she packed a small suitcase. She started crying as she sewed some of her jewelry into the inside of her clothes. This was a good way to carry them without risking losing them or having other people see them.

Inside she was aching. She was gripped by remorse that she was abandoning her family.

She was clinging to her memories.

At that moment, she realized she resented her father. She never earned a word of praise from him. She felt that she could not do anything right to please him. He always criticized her. Being such a strict father was the cause of her shyness and reclusion as a young child. He was not the type of father who would hug her or tell her he loved her.

She couldn't help wondering if her father wanted her to escape. If so, why did he want her to go? Was it because he wanted her to live in freedom? Or was it because he wanted her out of the way so he could have her mother all to himself?

Her mother always stood up for her. She was always on her side in just about anything and everything.

When Vera returned from England, she was more independent and started influencing her mother to be more independent. Vladimir resented this.

Regardless of her father's motives, he would always be in her heart.

Vera lay in bed in an agonizing agitation, thinking and thinking.

At midnight, Vera rose, washed her face with cold water, and walked down the corridor. She was sure her parents were asleep by now. It was impossible to think about anything but her escape.

As she tiptoed by her parents' bedroom she froze when she noticed a light under their door.

Did her parents hear her? She realized that her mother had probably fallen asleep while reading her book.

She descended the stairs quietly, not wanting to awaken her parents. She unlocked the front door and when she opened it, Stephan was standing there, hiding in the darkness of the entrance.

He stepped into the hall; she shut the door behind him.

Vera gave him a kiss.

"Darling, are you ready?" Stephan whispered.

Vera nodded her head as they tiptoed upstairs.

Afraid their voices might echo down in her parents' bedroom, they didn't say anything.

As they crossed the creaky wood floors, the creaking of the hardwood floors under their feet sounded very loud to them.

Vera's heart was racing and she felt a knot tighten in her stomach. Her legs were trembling.

Once inside her bedroom she hugged and kissed Stephan. She was trying to find comfort in his arms. She needed reassurance that she was making the right decision.

Stephan looked into her eyes and said, "Everything

will be fine, my darling. You know your parents want the best for you…and that's your freedom."

XXIV

By daybreak, Vera and Stephan were able to get an early train and travel south to Kuty in Slovakia.

It had been raining all night and throughout the day.

They were to meet their prearranged guide, Guido, at the station.

Guido was in his late twenties, medium build, with dark hair. Both of his parents were Italian.

As they got off the train, Stephan saw that two of his friends were already there.

Stephan walked toward a tall blond guy, hugged him and said. "Hi, Karol, I'm glad you made it."

"Good to see you Stephan," said Karol.

"You remember Rudolph, don't you?" Rudolph was a Russian with very back hair, white skin, and blue eyes.

"Yes, I do. Hello, Rudolph." Stephan turned toward Vera and said. "This is my girlfriend, Veruska."

Guido interrupted their conversation. "Come...come quickly. I'm Guido. We need to start our journey thought the forest. The weather is so miserable with this rain and fog," he whispered as he quickly disappeared into the woods.

The fog and the drizzle made it impossible to see

anything in the forest.

"This fog is so intense, how do you know if we are going the right direction?" Vera asked. "We cannot see any visual landmarks or stars to guide us in the right direction and this wooded forest has dozens of unmapped hiking and hunting trails."

Guido smiled at Vera. "One way of telling where we are is to look at the trees. In Czechoslovakia, there are forests with common oaks of 130 to 140 feet tall. As one approaches Slovakia the forest is on extremely fertile soil, especially along the Danube River; therefore, the tree heights are 140 to164 feet, and the trunks are thicker."

Guido stopped for a second and looked Vera in the eyes. He could tell she wasn't too sure about him.

"Don't worry I know where we are going. I just hope this is the last rain of this season, so hopefully you will be able to see where we are once this storm pass through."

Vera smiled back at him. His confidence made Vera feel more comfortable with the idea that they were going in the right direction.

They had walked for nearly four hours when they felt tired and decided to take a break. It wasn't easy hiking in a muddy forest and carrying their suitcases.

They rested on a big rock and ate the sandwiches they had brought with them.

As Vera looked up, a small squirrel darted up the

branches of a beautiful tree. Looking at the small happy animal comforted her.

"Let's keep going—it looks like it going to start raining again," Guido said.

"Isn't this supposed to be the end of the rainy season?" Karol asked.

"Yes, the rainy season should be over by now." Guido smiled. "This has been an unusually wet season."

"Hopefully the rain will stop any minute now," Rudolph said, pointing to a patch of blue sky.

Five minutes later, a torrential rain began to fall, accompanied by lightning and thunder.

Hour after hour, the wind, the rain, thunder, and lightning continued scattering over them. The flashes of lighting got brighter and more intense while the thunder got louder.

It was like a small deluge descending on them. Their feet splashed through pools of muddy water. They could barely see anything in front of them. The sound of rain was all around them.

They were soaking wet and it was getting harder to carry their suitcases. They were totally exhausted, wet, and cold when they reached the barn.

"We are getting closer to the Austrian border. We will hide here during the day, and tomorrow night we will have to cross a small river and proceed into Austria. Hopefully, it will stop raining. You can sleep over there in the loft." Guido pointed to the barn full of cows.

All night they could hear the rain pounding relentlessly on the barn roof and the cows mooing below. Rats were everywhere. Vera could her them.

XXV

The next morning the rain was still coming down in buckets.

Vera was lying down in the loft, wondering how her parents had reacted when they found out what had happened. She had left a letter on top of her bed telling them that she was running away. She smiled sadly, wondering if she ever would see them again.

Many miles away, at Vera's parents' house, her parents stood at gunpoint and watched as Inspector Poděbrad snatched Vera's letter, read it, then threw Vera's letter on the floor and let out a roar of rage.

"Dammmm! I really must apologize, Mr. and Mrs. Pisova, for disturbing you, but I have to know where your daughter is right now."

"Inspector Poděbrad, the only information we have is in the letter that you just threw on the floor." Vladimir was staring at the letter on the floor.

"Have you heard from her?" Inspector Poděbrad demanded.

"No, we haven't." Vladimir was trying to stay calm.

"And," he said, "I suppose if you did hear from her, you would not tell me."

"That is my business, Inspector Poděbrad," Vladimir replied angrily.

"I already told you, the only information we have is what she wrote in the letter. Do you think I'm happy my only daughter has run away?"

"Let me warn you, she could be in deep trouble for helping Stephan, so if you hear from your daughter you had better convince her to come back. If she will help me capture Stephan, I will make sure that nothing happens to her because she helped with the capturing of an anti-party leader."

Vladimir was staring at Inspector Poděbrad thinking, *Why does the inspector keep saying Vera will be in deep trouble for helping Stephan? She is running away, not helping Stephan*

"By the way, Dr. Pisova," the inspector said with a sinister smile on his face, "two days ago, late afternoon, a police officer was in the process of arresting a man fitting Stephan's description. Everything was under control until he was attacked by a woman." He paused and looked at Vladimir.

Vladimir still looked puzzled.

"The woman who attacked the policeman was a young blonde female. Her description fits that of your daughter."

Babushka turned around toward the house and said. "I must go inside. I need something to drink…something strong like vodka."

"That's impossible! My daughter was here almost the entire day." Vladimir's eyes widened as he clenched his teeth.

"Was she here around between the hours of 7:00 and

8:00 p.m.?" The inspector asked. The tone of voice was very accusatory and suspicious.

"Yes, she arrived home at 5:30 p.m. I was here when she arrived." Vladimir's voice was firm.

Vera's mother was silent, staring at Vladimir because she knew Vera had returned long after curfew time.

"I have the feeling that you are not telling me the whole truth, Dr. Pisova."

Inspector Poděbrad looked skeptical as he turned and looked straight at Vera's mother. She started to panic and lowered her eyes toward the ground not waiting to make eye contact with him. She was scared to death of him.

Inspector Poděbrad smiled before he said, "We will catch them! I promise you."

Vladimir was visibly stunned and his deepest fear had just been confirmed...Vera and Stephan were now on the run from the police.

The bitch got away! Now they have left me no choice. I must catch her and Stephan, Inspector Poděbrad thought to himself while he drove back to the police station.

XXVI

Stephan, Vera, Karol, and Rudolph were confined to the large, damp, windowless barn all day long listening to the rain fall. It would not stop raining.

That evening, Guido walked into the barn and introduced them to Charles, the owner of the farm. Charles brought them sandwiches to eat. He was a short and stocky man, in his late forties, with white skin, blue eyes, and a baldhead. He was sympathetic to their determination to escape. He also knew he was putting his entire family at risk by helping them.

"In a few hours, after dark, we will leave here. We will cross the river and head for the Austrian border. The river that we are crossing is generally knee deep but with all this rain the waters will be higher; however, we should still be able to cross it." Guido smiled at them.

"Now that we have some free time, let me go over the rest of our plans." Guido started by admitting he had been engaged in smuggling contraband across the Alps since the end of World War II.

"So hopefully tonight we will get a break in this miserable weather and we will be able to cross the small river. From there we will be able to go on and cross the border into Austria. Karol and Rudolph are going west and they will meet one of their relatives who will help them."

Guido turned and looked at Stephan and Vera.

"You will go south and east following the Danube River. You will go through the 'Wiener Wald' woods and eventually you will end up in Vienna."

"Once in Vienna, go to the Astoria Hotel located on Kärntner Straße, just a few steps away from the State Opera House."

Stephan and Vera listened to Guido very carefully.

"You will register under the name of Mr. and Mrs. Alex Khatchadourian."

"There will be a package addressed in the name of Alex Khatchadourian. The package will contain two Austrian passports. The Austrian passports will need your signatures and your photos. Once you have your photos taken and affixed in the passports, all you have to do is to dampen this paper slightly and impress this stamp on it."

Guido handed him a metal disc, and said. "This is the embossing stamp of the Austrian government. After that is done, you just need to present yourselves as Austrians citizens." He laughed.

Vera put her arms around Stephan.

"We'll be leaving here soon. I want to cross the river before this other storm arrives," Guido said, pointing toward the black clouds coming their way.

They all smiled and waited until it was time for them to go.

It was late at night when they left the barn. It had stopped raining but the wind had started blowing. By the time they reached the river, the new storm had arrived. Guido looked at the river and realized that the small knee-deep stream had become a raging torrent. There was no way they were going to be able to cross it.

"I have never seen the waters in this river so high and so strong. There is no way we will be able to cross it tonight, especially now that this new storm has arrived."

The wind was getting stronger and they could hear from a distance the thunder from the approaching storm.

They walked in silence back to the barn. The air was so fresh and cold.

By the time they returned to the barn, it was pouring and they were soaking wet. The rain pelted their faces, making very hard to see.

From then on time dragged on. The combination of the rain and the anticipation of not knowing when they would be able to continue their journey plus not being able to go anywhere made things unbearable.

The next two days the rain continued coming down in buckets and each night they unsuccessfully tried crossing the river.

"Oh, my God! I cannot take all this rain, just sitting here waiting for the stupid rain to stop." Vera was so frustrated.

On their third night while attempting to cross the river,

they ran into another group staying in a barn closer to the river. Unable to cross again, they left their suitcases in that group's barn. That way they wouldn't have to carry them as far.

Once they returned to their barn, Guido decided to change the plans. "The longer we stay here the higher are the chances of getting caught. This rain is not going to stop for a few more days and the water will continue rising due to the runoff from the mountains. Tomorrow morning I am going to the next village, located on the banks of the Morava River. There I know someone who has a boat and I will ask him if we can borrow the boat so we can cross the river tomorrow night."

"Great idea!" Stephan said enthusiastically.

"I cannot believe we will be out of here." Vera had a big smile on her face.

"Oh no! I will miss this place, especially the cows." Karol laughed loudly.

"You can stay here." Rudolph grabbed Karol and started ticking him. "You are such a silly man."

The next morning, Guido left the barn very early to go the village.

As the hours went by, Stephan kept looking outside, hoping that Guido would be returning from the village.

By nightfall, with the rain still falling, Guido had not returned.

The four of them sat around the barn wondering when

Guido was coming back. They tried not to show their feelings of discouragement.

The following day, they realized that something had happened to Guido.

"Guido simply disappeared! I hope nothing happened to him." Stephan was very concerned.

They decided to wait until it stopped raining and then they would try crossing the river again. They were also hoping that Guido would return.

The following day, the barn door opened and Charles came running into the barn. He looked very scared.

"You must leave here immediately," Charles told them. "Please, leave now," he repeated.

"But...why?" Vera asked.

"My sister works for the police department and she overheard the caption mention that someone in the village had denounced Guido to a police officer. A truckload of police are searching the village and all the farms around here. They have already arrested one group who were staying in a barn closer to the river." There was a desperate tone to his voice.

Stephan and Vera looked at each other, wondering if that was the group they had met two nights before, the ones they left their suitcases with.

"They brought in another inspector to help them with the arrests. He arrived from Prague yesterday."

"Prague?" Stephan asked the farmer.

"Yes! And he has a horrible reputation." The farmer quivered.

"Do you know his name?" Vera asked quickly.

"No," the farmer answered.

"Supposedly it all started when someone told the inspector about a judge in Prague who was helping political prisoners and others escape."

"You said a Czech judge in Prague?" Stephan asked.

"Yes."

"Do you remember the judge's name?" Was it Milosh?" Stephan was staring at the farmer and holding his breath.

"Yes! That's him. Just before they were going to arrest this judge, he committed suicide rather than face imprisonment."

"Oh, my God!" Vera's voice was shaky.

Suddenly Stephan got up. He was trying not to panic. "Charles is right. We need to go." Stephan's brain was racing all over the place. He started to feel that everything was falling apart. *This is not happening to me, I cannot panic; otherwise, this will be the end of us,* he thought to himself.

"They will be looking for us. We must get over the border into Austria as soon as possible. Every minute we lose, the more danger we are in." He paused for a second. "The inspector who came from Prague has to be Inspector Poděbrad. He will stop at nothing until he captures us. The group arrested yesterday is probably the same group with whom we left our suitcases. Once they open our suitcases they will know that they are very close to capturing us," Stephan said.

There was silence among them.

"And if he captured Guido he will extract our plans from him and he will probably wait for us at the river."

"So what are we going to do?" Karol asked Stephan.

A feeling of panic came over him. "I don't know—let me think." Stephan couldn't think, he was totally overwhelmed by the situation.

Charles started to plead with Stephan again. "Please, I beg you. You must leave immediately. If you get caught here, my family and I will suffer horrible consequences."

"It's all over! I cannot think of another solution. Even if we continued with our plans we don't have a boat to cross the river." Stephan felt defeated.

"No! There is no way that we are giving up!" Vera said loudly.

"We cannot go back! We have come this far, I refuse to just let him capture us. Everything that you have been fighting for would mean nothing." Vera was staring at Stephan. "Darling, don't give up. Isn't there another way to get into Austria from here? There has to be another way," Vera pleaded.

For the first time she understood exactly what Stephan been fighting for.

There was a moment's hesitation and then Stephan

said, "You are right! We are not giving up. Let me think about this, there has to be a way."

A few minutes later, Stephan started to think out loud. "We know we cannot continue going in this direction because I have the suspicion Inspector Poděbrad and his men are probably waiting to capture us. Even if Inspector Poděbrad is not at the river, he will be searching all the farms. We know also that right now we cannot cross the river so the longer we wait the greater are our chances of being caught."

Stephan looked at all of them, waiting to see if anyone had any ideas. He knew they had to plot their next move very quickly.

"Well, I have only one option that I can think of...we'll go back to Kuty and catch a train to Bratislava. Once we get there, we will walk approximately ten miles following the Danube River until we get to Devin Castle ruins. That is where the Danube is the narrowest and we can try getting across the river into Austria."

"Do you mean swimming across to Austria?" Rudolph asked.

"Yes, that is the only way I know to cross into Austria. It is not going to be easy because the Devin ruins are under military occupation. The river is under surveillance by Communist armed border guards. Those armed guards are charged with preventing anyone from escaping into Austria.

More than three hundred people have been shot dead trying to escape to the West. We will need to watch the guards—our timing must be perfect."

Stephen continued, "Well, if we agree with this plan we better move out of here now."

They all nodded agreement.

"All right then, let's go," Rudolph said.

"God be with you," the farmer told them.

A few miles away Inspector Poděbrad and his men were combing all houses, looking for Stephan and Vera.

We already caught Guido and one group. In a few more hours I will capture and get rid of Stephan Lucas and Vera Pisova, Inspector Poděbrad told himself.

XXVII

Just as the four of them were leaving the barn and walking into the forest, a truckload of policemen descended on Charles's farm.

The weather was drizzling and very foggy, making it easy for the four of them to get from the barn into the forest and not been seen.

Stephan hoped they could remember how to get back to Kuty train station.

The forest was dark and very muddy from all the rain. They could hear the crunch of the grass and mud under their feet and occasionally the cracking branches, which sounded very loud.

In the distance, they could hear the policemen searching the farms.

They walked in silence, scared and unsure of themselves.

"Ahhhh! Oh, my God, I hate this." Vera started jumping around and waving her hands in front of her face. "I hate spider webs."

Stephan came closer to help clear her face.

"Thank you, darling. Please walk in front of me."

Stephan smiled and kissed her.

They walked for another two hours. They were feeling tired and cold. Vera's feet were cold and wet from all the muddy water spilling into her shoes.

I should just go back to my parents' house. This is crazy. We will probably be killed trying to escape or will end up in jail anyway. Or perhaps we would have been better off taking our chances and letting Inspector Poděbrad arrest Stephan. This way Stephan could tell him that he had no connection with the car bombing attempt..."

Suddenly her thoughts were interrupted as she screamed again.

"Ahhhhh!" At that point, the muddy soil gave way beneath her feet and she fell to the ground.

"Darling, are you OK?" Stephan asked, as he helped her to her feet.

"Yes, I am, just hold me, please." Vera forced a small smile.

"Don't give up. We will make it," Stephan mumbled as he embraced and kissed her.

Tears filled Vera's eyes.

They had walked another hour when Karol said, "We should already have reached Kuty. Are we sure we are going in the right direction?"

"Relax! Yes, we are going the right direction. Look over there, I can see some houses," Stephan answered proudly.

"Now we must get back to the train station without the police seeing us." Stephan said when they reached the city.

They made their way to the train station. Rudolph decided he would walk around the station and take a look.

"Be very careful," Karol told him as he hugged him.

"I will." Rudolph smiled back at him.

Twenty minutes later, Rudolph returned. "The police are everywhere and they are checking everyone's identification."

"What are we going to do now?" Vera asked.

"I checked and the next train to Bratislava leaves in half an hour from platform 2," Rudolph said. "Next to the platform 2, there is a small lost and found room. It has an exit door going to the street. You wait on the street while I go into the lost and found room. Hopefully, it will be so busy that I will be able open the door to let you in. From there we can make a dash to the train, hopefully without the policemen seeing us."

Half an hour later, they moved quickly though the lost and found room and managed to board the train. They were now on their way to Bratislava.

XXVIII

They got off in Bratislava and quickly made their way into the forest going west toward Devin Castle ruins.

Though they were exhausted, they knew they had another ten miles to go. They walked all day in the rain.

"This damn weather!" Vera exclaimed. "I'm exhausted and cold from walking in this rain. I hope we are getting closer because I don't know how longer I can go."

"I know but we should be approaching Devin Castle soon." Stephan tried to sound confident. "Let me tell you a little about the Devin Castle history; hopefully, it will distract you from our journey."

"The only thing that will distract me from this would be a nice shower and a very comfortable bed," Vera responded quickly.

"The oldest settlement of Devin dates all the way to the Stone Age. The Celtic and then the Romans came in, making Devin a strategic outpost for those legions."

Stephan put his arm around Vera.

"The Slavs arrived during the sixth century AD. Prince Rastislav of Great Moravia, an incredible strategic thinker, realized it was the perfect place to defend the central part of Great Moravia By early 1600 Devin was one of the greatest castles in that region. It had become an impenetrable citadel, firmly rooted into a cliff high above the confluence of the Danube and Morava rivers. In 1809, Napoleon saw no use for Devin Castle, and his army destroyed this magnificent castle."

Stephan turned to Vera and kissed her. "So, my darling, as you can see, you will be overnight in one of the greatest castles in Europe."

"You are so good to me."

They walked another three miles, surrounded by darkness. They were exhausted, hungry, and they started to wonder if they were going the right direction.

Suddenly, Stephan screamed. "I see it." He pointed into the dark. "It is over there! Do you see it?" They all looked in the same direction.

"I can't see anything. Are you sure?" Rudolph asked.

"Vera squinted her eyes. "I don't see anything."

"I swear I saw it," Stephan said with confidence.

"I think we are all tired and perhaps we are starting to see things." Karol also couldn't see the castle. "I have to sit down and rest my tired legs."

They all sat on the ground staring at the horizon surrounded by darkness in the dead silence of the night. Once in a while the sky would light up from lighting from another approaching storm.

They remained silent, trying to regain some strength and confidence.

Suddenly, like magic, the clouds separated and the

rays from a gigantic full moon shone across the surface of the Danube River.

Projected on the dark waters they could see the magnificent reflection of the ruins of the castle. This majestic ruins were sitting on a huge towering rock formation on the end of the cliff overlooking the Danube River.

"Look! It is so beautiful." Vera was mesmerized by the reflection.

They all hugged each other as the expressions on their faces changed and they felt relief knowing where they were.

"Let's keep going," Stephan said. "We still must climb up the cliff and there is another storm approaching very quickly. We'll spend the night in the ruins and tomorrow we will go down to the river and get across to Austria."

They started climbing the steep hill. They could hear the thunder getting louder from the approaching storm that was coming straight at them.

The climb became steeper and more difficult.

The ground was very slippery from so much rain, making the climb very hard. They moved slowly against the fierce wind.

Suddenly, the dark skies started unleashing Mother Nature's full force.

Flashes of lighting brought daylight to the trees.

Everyone looked scared as the wind picked up. The

earth seemed to tremble with each thunder clap. Each step was getting harder and harder and they were getting wet.

"This damn weather!" Stephan yelled.

It felt like they were at war, with bombs falling everywhere.

The thunder was so loud that Vera could not hear Stephan. He gestured for them to run toward a grove of trees.

As they started to run, huge raindrops started to fall on them. It felt like someone was throwing small rocks at them.

Stephan pulled Vera a few yards under the tress while Rudolph and Karol ran in the opposite direction.

There was an immense deluge of water coming down on them. In matter of a few seconds, they were absolutely drenched.

At the same time, an avalanche of water, mud, and rocks came crashing down the cliff barely missing them.

The skies gave another roar and suddenly a powerful blinding light descended right next to them. A lightning bolt had slit open the tree next to them. They could feel the heat against their skin and sense a burning smell.

At the same time, half of the burning tree came crashing down right in front of them.

"Ahhhh! Oh, my God!" Vera screamed. At the same time, dirt and rocks started flying everywhere.

Stephan could feel the ground moving from under him as he tried holding on to Vera. His body fell on top of her. They could feel debris falling down on them. It felt as if a grenade had just exploded in front of them.

"I can't see anything," Vera yelled at Stephan as they were temporary blinded by the brightness of the lightning.

"Just keep lying down; the storm is too strong for us to do anything." His fingers dug into the dirt in case something else would pull them down the cliff.

"Grab onto me and don't let go. Keep your eyes closed. They probably were burned from looking at the lightning."

The storm lasted for another fifteen minutes.

Stephan could feel Vera's body trembling under his.

Once the storm was gone, Karol and Rudolph came running over. Rudolph extended his hand and pulled Stephan and Vera out of the mud. Their vision was still blurred.

They knew they had to continue up the cliff. The path became narrow and very zigzaggy. They heard the sound of rainwater running down the cliff as well as the sound of their feet splashing through pools of muddy water.

Occasionally they could still see lightning in the distance.

As they were approaching the top of the cliff, they had to climb along a very narrow ledge, holding on to the weeds and sparse grass that grew in the dirt between the rocks. After an hour of hard work, they managed to reach the top.

They simply threw themselves into the dirt at the edge of the cliff. They were exhausted and soaking wet.

"Let's keep going," Stephan told them.

A few minutes later, with the wind still fierce, they entered the ruins.

A very small footpath led them up the hill past a wooden shelter. On the right were the ruins of a Roman settlement. As they continued climbing the path, they wound up around to a wooden drawbridge leading to the main courtyard.

"Let's overnight over there." Stephan pointed to the lone tower on the jagged cliff.

They stood in total darkness on the edge of the cliff. They were exhausted and trembling, not so much because of the cold wind, but afraid of the darkness and the uncertainness of the future.

They could hear and feel the breeze generated by the Danube River below.

Stephan pulled Vera next to him. "Darling, can you feel the breeze coming from below us? It is being generated by the famous Danube River. No other river in the entire world has inspired so many poets, musicians, and painters to create so many masterpieces. Just imagine, this famous river flows past mighty castles, historic cities, magnificent architecture, and so many different cultural treasures. Right over there in the dark, across the river, is the farmland of Austria...The gateway to our freedom." Stephan smiled.

"Yes! And once we are across the river it will be the

beginning of our new lives," Vera whispered, trying to sound as confident as Stephan. "Let's get some rest. We will need it for tomorrow."

They walked down a set of stairs leading to the castle's innards, revealing a dank dungeon of a room.

"Well, here are our accommodations—a perfect prison cell or, if you prefer, a torture chamber." Stephan gave a sinister laugh.

"We should stay together, taking turns keeping guard. I'll go first," Karol said, as he collapsed of exhaustion on the floor.

There was a brief silence.

"Everything is so quiet. You can even hear someone's soul wondering around the ruins," Rudolph whispered, sending a chill through everyone's body.

"Oh, thanks! Now I will really be able to sleep." Vera looked at Rudolph.

They all laughed.

A few minutes went by and suddenly the silence was broken. "Booooooooooo!" Stephan screamed.

"Oh, my God, are you trying to kill us?" Karol screamed.

"That wasn't funny." Vera slapped Stephan's head.

They started laughing again.

Vera pinned Stephan down and kissed his lips.

"I want you to hold me in your arms...I want to fall

sleep like this." Vera curled herself up in Stephan's arms. *I know I'm in love with him and I know I made the right decision,* she told herself.

In the other corner of the room, Rudolph was holding Karol and telling him. "I love having you next to me. You make me feel secure...This is the beginning of a new life and I want you to be part of my new life...Great things will start happening for us, you will see."

A few minutes later, the only sounds that one could hear were the splashing waters of the Danube and the wind howling around the castle ruins.

XXVIX

Just before dawn, the sky cleared and moonlight shone on the rippling waters of the Danube River. The combination of the shining waters and the surrounding hillsides formed an enchanting landscape.

The darkness was turning to mist. Stephan had his arms around Vera as they watched the sun slowly rise over the river.

In the other corner, Rudolph and Karol were also looking at the sunrise.

All four kept staring at the rising sun and beautiful landscape. Everything looked so peaceful and harmonious it was easy to wish that the feeling of happiness and security would not go away.

Some time passed before they started walking around. Their spirits were lifted after looking at such a magnificent sight.

It had been a long time since the sun shone so brightly, welcoming the arrival of spring. They could smell the fragrance of spring in the air.

"Let's go down to the beach just below the ruins. That is where the Danube and Morava rivers merge and the water flows faster. If you look over there, you will see that the water from the Morava River is much darker compared to the blue

Danube. We'll pretend to be sunbathing, four innocent young students enjoying the first day of spring." Stephan took a deep breath, hoping his plan was going to work.

They made their way down the cliff, through a little wooded area, to a small stone beach on which they pretended to be spending the day.

"This is a perfect location," Stephan said. "We have a good view of the constant river traffic. Once we are in the water we will have to swim quickly, as the current takes us downstream and, at the same time, watch not to be run down by the boats and barges carrying merchandising and passengers."

Stephan continued, "If you look up you can see two guards patrolling the riverfront." As they looked up, the two uniformed guards had stopped to salute a superior.

"We must time them. Each guard patrols a given distance. When two guards meet they about-face and march back to the other end of their area, meet another guard, again about-face and repeat their march. As you will see, at one point both guards will be out of sight. That is when we make our way into the river and can be far enough across so that when the guards return they will not spot us."

They listened to Stephan while they pretended to be lying down to get some sun and enjoy themselves.

"We have to time the guards for a while, so our timing

must be perfect."

"Hey! You are blocking my sun," Vera said as she giggled.

"What?" Stephan asked.

"I'm just an innocent young girl enjoying a day at the beach." Vera laughed and hugged Stephan. She was trying to hide her fear.

After so much rain, Vera was enjoying the warm breeze blowing on her face.

Karol and Rudolph also looked worried. "There are so many boats going up and down this river." Karol was looking at Stephan.

"Yes, that is why our timing must be perfect."

"The water is moving fast, and the current looks so strong, it will pull us toward the center of the river. Can we really swim across to Austria?" Rudolph appeared the most vulnerable of the four.

"We'll make it." Stephan was trying to sound confident. "Let's start timing the guards."

The next few hours they spent observing and timing the guards and looking at the river traffic. They went over their plan step-by-step many times.

"This is it...the next time the guards are out of sight we will jump into the water and swim cross to Austria. Just remember to keep going, don't look back, timing is critical. Try swimming low in the water without splashing too much water. If you are in trouble and need help, raise your arm to the same level as your head. Don't raise your hands too high; you don't want to draw the guard's attention." Stephan's voice was confident.

"Good luck." Rudolph's voice was shaky.

All four sat in a circle, holding hands, waiting for the soldiers to disappear from sight.

Vera's heart was pounding so fast that she started to tremble with fear.

Stephan reached out and took her in his arms.

"Are you all right?"

Vera nodded as she forced a smile.

Suddenly, Stephan said, "They are gone! Let's go." He ran toward the water.

Rudolph looked at the water, "Are we sure we can make it? The river is flowing extremely fast....Oh well, God, please help us get across..." he said as he jumped into the water.

Vera was wearing her expensive leather coat and was determined not to part with it. "Wait a moment, I'm tying my coat around my waist."

Stephan wasn't listening to what she was saying, he had already plunged into the Danube, fully clothed.

He keep looking back to make sure the guards had not returned.

"Veruska, hurry up, we only have a few minutes before the guards return."

"I'm coming!" Vera had finished tying her coat around her waist.

"Brrrrr, this water is so cold." Vera jumped into the water. It was the critical time to start swimming.

A few feet from shore Vera started to panic, as she realized the leather coat had become waterlogged and was pulling her under. Vera went under the water as she tried untying her coat. The coat was incredibly heavy so she had to let it go.

She came above the surface, looked ahead, and saw the others way in front of her risking their lives waiting for her.

Vera waived to them that she was all right and for them to continue swimming.

The first few minutes she really didn't have to swim—she let the current carry her toward the middle of the river. She only prayed that they would not be run down by one of the boats going up and down the river.

The Danube River is the second largest river in Europe. It is the main artery of transportation for big barges and passenger boats as it crosses Austria, Germany, Croatia, Slovakia, Hungary, Serbia, Romania, and Bulgaria before emptying into the Black Sea.

As Vera neared the middle of the river, she started swimming as fast as she could, working her way toward the Austrian shore.

She suddenly realized the river was flowing extremely fast and the current was getting stronger. She was being pulled away from the shore.

All of a sudden, Vera felt everything was going in slow motion. She could hear boat engine motors under the water. Every stroke she took seemed like an eternity.

Vera's legs and arms were getting very tired and they started to cramp.

She went under the water for a few seconds, but after a few kicks, she managed to get her head above the water. She was gasping for breath.

She knew she had to reach the shore now; otherwise, she would not make it. Once she went around the bend in the river, it would be impossible for her to reach the shore because the current would get even stronger and faster.

After what seemed an eternity, Vera was finally close to the shore. She knew she had to find the strength to make it.

She looked at the shore and thought, *Come, you can make it. Just remember, you are swimming toward your freedom. Where is Stephan? I don't see him. I hope he made it safely to the shore.* Vera had been pulled a long distance downstream from where they started.

Her hands managed to grab a small tree branch. She

was hanging over the water. Ten seconds later, the branch broke. She took a deep breath just before she went under the water.

The turbulent waters were pulling her down and away from the shore.

I'm not going to make it, I'm too tired and my legs are cramping. God, just let me die quickly. Let the river take me for good, Vera thought.

Suddenly out of nowhere, someone grabbed her right hand, which was the only part of her body above the water.

"Come on, you are almost there!" Stephan screamed.

He barely had a hold of her hand. They knew his grip was too weak—she was slipping down into the water again.

For a split second, it took all of Vera's strength to lift her left arm and grab Stephan's hand.

The next thing Vera remembered were her legs hitting the water but her upper body hitting land. She felt her ribs being jabbed by the rocks.

She suddenly realized Stephan had pulled her to shore. He had his arms around her. She was trembling and started to cry.

She had made it.

XXX

For a few seconds, Vera lay on the shore, breathing heavily, not moving. Her eyes were closed as if she was dead. She was overcome by physical and emotional fatigue.

She felt the earth under her, realizing she was alive. It was such a wonderful feeling. She smiled. *I'm alive, thank you, God,* she told herself.

Vera knew that by no means was she free, they were still in the Russian Zone of Austria and therefore still in danger of being caught. At that moment it didn't matter to her; she just wanted to treasure that intense feeling of being alive.

She opened her eyes. Stephan had his arms around her and was staring at her.

"My darling, you made it."

"You saved my life. You are so wonderful." Vera could feel her teeth chattering. There were so many feelings and emotions inside of her.

She started sobbing uncontrollably as all those feelings were coming out.

"I'm fine, just give me a moment. I just need to let it all out."

"My silly girl, let it all out!" Stephan said to Vera before kissing her.

Suddenly, they heard approaching footsteps coming from

the bushes behind them.

"Stephan!" Vera jumped and whispered. "Someone is coming."

"Stop right there! You are under arrest!" a voice screamed.

Both of them froze.

This cannot be happening to us...not after what we went through...Please, God! Vera thought.

"You are under arrest!" a voice called very loudly.

"Yes, you are under arrest for kissing in Austria," Another voice called.

There was a brief silence and then Karol and Rudolph started laughing.

"Oh, my God! That wasn't funny!" Vera's heartbeat had jumped.

"What isn't funny is the fact that you are here kissing and could care less about us. We could have been dead and it wouldn't have mattered," Karol whispered.

"Karol, didn't you hear them calling while they were kissing? They were calling, Karol! Rudolph! Where are you? We need to find them."

There was silence for a moment and then they all burst out laughing, before hugging each other.

"Well, we all made it!" Vera exclaimed.

"I almost didn't make it. The distance and the current were too much for me. Karol had to help me." Rudolph hugged Karol.

"We should be going. Our first task is to seclude ourselves and dry our sopping clothes. Once we are dry, we have to make our way on foot to the nearest train station to go to Vienna. We must move quickly; we don't want to raise any suspicions."

"Let's hide over there behind those bushes and dry our sopping clothes."

Stephan turned to Vera and gave her his jacket. "My darling, take this, I don't want you to be cold. We know how easily you get cold, especially now that you don't have your coat. I hope you didn't lose too much when you let go of the coat." Stephan was looking at Vera.

"I have most of my jewelry sewn inside my underwear and the little I had in my coat I was able to grab and put in my pocket before letting the coat go," Vera said, proudly.

While the clothes were drying, Stephan went for a walk to look around. As the sun was going to set very soon, Stephan thought it best for them to overnight somewhere close. They were simply exhausted.

Half an hour later, Stephan rejoined the group.

"I think it would be a good idea for us to overnight around here. It will soon be dark and we don't know this area. We can continue tomorrow morning after our bodies and minds get some rest. Agreed?"

Vera was so exhausted from her swim, she just

wanted to stay lying on the ground, eyes closed, without having to think of anything.

Rudolph and Karol, each with a sad face, looked at each other.

"What's wrong?" Stephan asked.

"I wish the circumstances would be different so we could stay here and enjoy each other's company but we still have a long way to go to freedom. We are going across Austria, through the Alps, and then make our way into Italy. We still can catch a late train tonight. I don't want to travel by train during the day; there are too many soldiers around."

"I don't blame you. Well, my dear friends, here is where we say good-bye." Stephan hugged Karol, held him very tight. That was probably the last time they would see each other.

"I will miss you so much, just do me a favor, and be very careful." Vera had opened her eyes and stood up.

"Good luck and thanks for everything," Rudolph said as he hugged them.

"I wish you were coming with us." Vera's eyes were teary.

Rudolph and Karol smiled and left, waving to them before disappearing into the fields.

Stephan and Vera stared after them for a while, and then walked the opposite direction. Tears were coming down Vera's face.

"There is a small farm with a barn around that bend, a good place for us to overnight. The barn is not that close to the farmhouse and is near a forest...in case we need to escape."

They waited after dark until the lights at the farmhouse went off, then they made their way into the barn.

"What is this horrible smell?" Vera covered her nose.

"Well, we are not sleeping alone, we have some company. We will be sleeping with the pigs." Stephan laughed softly.

"Good heavens! I am suffocating with the smell of those creatures." Vera was trying to get used to the smell.

They found a small space where they could sleep. They lay down on straw, and Stephan put his arms around Vera to keep her warm. A minute later, she was sound asleep.

Vera was happy and felt safe with Stephan. It didn't matter where they were.

XXXI

Stephan wasn't able to sleep too well. He wanted to make sure they were up and out before the farmer came to the barn.

The pigs were all standing at the barn door as they were leaving.

"Well, my piggy friends, thank you so much for your hospitality. We must go now," Stephan mumbled.

"If one day I'm in this neighborhood again, I promise I will bring you a few bottles of perfume." Vera was covering her nose again.

Stephan smiled at her.

They made their way to the nearest town with a train station. They waited for the perfect timing to board the train to Vienna.

While seated on the train they kept a lookout for anyone asking to see identification.

To Vera, the roar and rattle of the train felt like being one step closer to a new life...a life of freedom and happiness with Stephan.

As the train stopped at each station, they were careful not to seen by anyone, specially the policemen standing outside on the platform.

"Look, darling! We are in Vienna," Stephan said as the train started to slow down.

A second later, he looked preoccupied.

"What's wrong?"

"We are changing our plans. I just have a feeling that Inspector Poděbrad and his men may be waiting to catch us at that hotel. I'm sure he was able to piece things together with the information he got from Judge Milosh's home, Guido, and the group who were arrested. When they arrested that group they also found our suitcases and inside my suitcase was a piece of paper with the name of the hotel where we were to stay here in Vienna and the Austrian passport stamp."

"So what are we going to do?"

"First, we should check into another hotel, somewhere here, close to the station." Stephan kissed and hugged Vera as they walked out of the train station.

"After that I will make a few phone calls to some of the contacts I was able to establish on my first escape."

At that moment, Vera realized that she had very strong feelings for Stephan. He was her hero. If it hadn't been for his intuition on who to trust and his knowledge and contacts they would never have made it that far. In her eyes, he was her leader and her guide.

"You know you are incredible? You seem to know how and when to make all the right moves." Vera was staring into Stephan's eyes and she wanted to make love to him right then.

"I am only using my contacts and experience from my first escape." Stephan's face was serious.

"Don't be so modest!"

"Veruska," Stephan took a deep breath, "I love you so much."

Vera smiled. "I...I love you too."

They kissed deeply.

"Let's go find a room."

Vera started to laugh.

"What? Not for that. You are always thinking about sex. We need to get some rest. Well..." Stephan had a smirk on his face. "If it happens, that is fine with me. Actually, it might make me sleep much better." Stephan laughed.

Vera needed to know her parents were all right so she decided to call her parents from one of the phone booths close to the station.

She dialed the number and waited for someone to answer. She could feel her heart beating very fast.

"Hello." Vladimir had answered the phone.

"Hello? Hello! Anyone there?" He paused for a second.

"Veruska, is that you? Speak to me!" Somehow Vladimir had the feeling that it might be his daughter.

There was some silence before Vera started speaking.

"Father," Vera said, "dear Father! Humm...I...I am on

my way. I just wanted to let you know we are all right so far."

"My little Veruska…"

"I'm sorry if I have made your life so miserable. Sorry I'm such a disgrace," she murmured.

Vera and Vladimir knew that the phone booth was private and safe, but the lines back home weren't. Anyone could be listening to their conversation, especially now that she was on the run.

When you picked up the phone receiver, the line was never clear. You could always hear other voices. You never said anything important or incriminating over the phone.

"Veruska, don't talk! Don't worry about anything. We are fine, be strong and brave." As usual there was calmness and firmness in Vladimir's voice.

Suddenly Vera could hear her mother on the background yelling, "Who is that? Is that Veruska?"

She knew she shouldn't talk anymore.

"I need to go."

"Oh, Veruska! My child! My little girl!"

"I love you!" Vera said, as she put the receiver down and started to sob.

"This is dreadful!" Vera said, looking at Stephan.

"I know but we must keep going," Stephan said as he grabbed her hand and they started to walk.

After walking around the station area for half an hour, they found a small, cheap and obscure hotel in a narrow street off the Place de Brouckere.

They settled in their room. Vera was totally exhausted and lay on the bed while Stephan made a few phone calls.

She was sound asleep when Stephan put his arm around her and whispered, "Darling, I have some good news. I have arranged to meet a few of my contacts." Stephan smiled. "Keep your fingers crossed. Hopefully, I will be able to get our documents so we can get through the Russian Zone and safely to Salzburg."

Stephan sounded confident. "Salzburg is the principal base operation of the IRO."

"The IRO?"

"Yes, the International Refugee Organization. They will help us find a new home."

"When are you meeting them?"

Stephan looked at his old watch that had been a gift from his parents days before they were assassinated.

"I must leave here in the next few minutes."

"Do you want me to come with you?"

"No, I want you to stay here. It could be dangerous."

"For the love of God, be careful." Vera's voice was concerned. "How long are you going to be gone?"

"A couple of hours, I should be back around 3:00 p.m." Stephan embraced and kissed her.

"Don't worry, darling, I'll be careful."

Vera smiled.

.

Vera couldn't go back to sleep. With each passing hour, Vera felt her confidence decreasing.

By 4:30 p.m., Vera was getting very worried. *What is taking him so long? What if something happened to Stephan? What should I do? Stop it, don't start panicking. Now is not the time to be frightened.*

Vera nervously paced around the room. She got tired of looking at the ugly padded nylon bedcover and the old television on the dresser opposite to the bed.

I'm going crazy in this room. Vera decided to go downstairs and have a drink that would relax her and make the time go by faster.

"May I have a vodka on the rocks with a twist?" she asked the bartender.

"Sure."

Vera finished her drink, paid the bill, went thought the lobby, and headed upstairs. As she stepped out of the elevator, she saw Stephan walking toward her in the hallway.

Vera ran to him and hugged him.

"I have been so worried. It is so late. I was going crazy. I feared that something went wrong. What happened? Did everything go all right? Are you all right? Did you meet with them?" Her questions poured out.

"My darling, slow down." Stephan kissed her. "Let's go

to our room."

Once inside their room, Stephan took off his jacket, grabbed Vera and they fell on top of the bed.

"It was nearly a disaster! First, I went to the hotel where we were supposed to stay and I was right, Inspector Poděbrad was waiting for us."

"Oh, my God. He will stop at nothing," Vera said, as she hugged Stephan and waited for him to continue telling her what had happened.

"With a small cash payment I was able to convince a young man to go to the lobby of the hotel and pretend to be Alex Khatchadourian. He was going to get the package addressed in that name and bring it to me. The minute the poor man mentioned Alex Khatchadourian, he was surrounded and questioned by Inspector Poděbrad. Once the young man told him I was across the street waiting for him to return, Inspector Poděbrad blew his whistle. That was a signal for his men to come out of hiding and capture me. Every building had undercover police who came out of hiding, looking for me."

Stephan held Vera's hand and looked into her eyes. "They came very close in capturing me. I'm only here because I was very lucky and I was able to convince an old lady that she needed help carrying her packages up to her apartment on the fifth floor. After leaving her apartment, I walked up to the roof of the building and was able to jump to the roof of the next building. From there I exited the building a block from the hotel."

"My poor darling, I was so worried about you." Vera's face was serious.

Stephan realized how lucky he was to escape. "We are going to take a break from the world. I'm ordering champagne for us. You and I are all that matters tonight."

The rest of that evening they pretended to be free. Nothing else mattered except their carnal desire for each other. They make love all night long.

Meanwhile, Inspector Poděbrad was furious with the events of that afternoon. He was going to search every hotel in Vienna until he found Stephan. He wanted him dead—nothing else mattered.

XXXII

During the following week, Stephan used his contacts and experiences from his first escape trying to get the documents they needed to travel out of Vienna.

Stephan and Vera were extremely careful not to call attention to themselves, going out only when they needed to do so. They were sure Inspector Poděbrad was still in the city looking for them.

One afternoon Stephan came back, running into their room, "Darling, where are you?"

Vera was standing in front of the window looking out the window.

"What's wrong?" She turned pale.

Stephan grabbed her and lifted her into the air.

"What are you doing?" Vera asked.

"We got them! Here are our new documents. We are now officially Austrian citizens. We can now get through the Russian Zone and into Salzburg."

"You are kidding, right?"

"No, look, here they are." Stephan was holding two passports.

"Stephan, you are so wonderful. I love you," Vera replied.

"I love you so much, but you already know that." Stephan smiled.

"Come on. We're getting on the next train out of here."

They walked to the train station and, once inside, Stephan raised his eyes and looked at the departure board.

"Damn! We only have ten minutes to buy our tickets and board the train…the last train today to Salzburg."

"What are we going to do? There is no way we can do that, take a look at all the people standing in line to buy tickets." Vera pointed to the long line ahead of them.

"No, it is going to be up to you for us to catch this train." Stephan said, smiling.

Vera had a puzzled look on her face. "I'm sorry? What do you mean?"

Stephan turned to her and said. "Come on, darling. You are beautiful and you can be very charming so work that magic to get to the front of the line. I'll stay here and wait for you."

"You are impossible!" Vera frowned as she ran to the back of the line and started working her charm.

"Excuse me, sir! Would you mind if I cut in front of you? Please help me. I have less than five minutes to catch my train. I must be on the next train. My mother is very sick and I am afraid she will not make it. Please, I beg you…Thank you very much."

Vera moved to the next person in front of her. "Excuse me. Miss, would you please…"

It took Vera less than five minutes to get to the ticket window and purchase their tickets. She grabbed the tickets and they started running toward the platform.

In the distance, they could hear the train engines start wheezing in preparation for departure. As the train started to pull away from the platform, they grabbed onto the last cart and pulled themselves aboard.

Meanwhile, Inspector Poděbrad and his men had just walked into the train station looking for them. One of the people working at the hotel front desk remembered seeing Stephan when he was checking out. He told the inspector that they were on their way to the train station.

Once again, he was furious as he realized that he had missed the train that had just left for Salzburg. There was one more chance for him to capture Stephan. He needed to make a phone call.

Inside the train, Stephan and Vera scanned the crowd and tried to stay out of sight.

They sat in the back of the car and Stephan opened a newspaper and pretended to be reading it.

Vera closed her eyes while feeling the motion of the wheels pounding on the tracks as the train picked up speed thought the dark night. The train followed the Danube River and the moon's reflection was shining on the clean and crispy waters coming down from the glacier. On the left was the silhouette of the mountains.

Stephan and Vera could not help themselves; they started to feel ecstatic. They knew they could still be caught but they were on their way to their final destination.

After a few hours, everything seemed to be going extremely well when all of a sudden the train slowed and stopped in the middle of the bridge over the Enns River in the town of Linz.

Russian soldiers were coming through the train interrogating passengers and examining their documents. Those suspected of having falsified documents were taken off the train. If, in fact, their documents were falsified, they would be prosecuted and sent to prison. They were also looking for political criminals or anarchists trying to escape. They had received special instructions from Inspector Poděbrad in Vienna asking to look for Stephan and Vera whom he strongly believed to be on that train.

Vera turned pale.

After a few minutes, the door to their car opened and three Russian soldiers asked the passengers to be ready to show them their tickets and passports.

Vera was nearly in tears, she was certain that the soldiers would detect that they were Czech, not Austrian.

She looked out the window, wondering if it would be

possible for them to survive jumping from the bridge into the river. It was too high; there was no way to survive the fall. There was no means of escape.

Her mind was working furiously as she looked around for a means of escape.

As the soldiers made their way toward them, Vera turned to Stephan and whispered, "Give me your glasses quickly."

She grabbed his glasses and bent the frame.

"What? What the hell are you doing? Those are my favorite glasses."

"Sorry, just listen to me, I have a plan." Vera cut him short. "I don't have time to explain." Vera could see in the corner of her eye that one of the soldiers was approaching them. "Don't say anything. Let me do all the talking so you know what I'm planning," Vera whispered as she put the crooked glasses on his face and mussed up his hair.

Her back was turned toward the soldier.

"Good evening. Can I see some identification?" the soldier asked Vera.

"Hello there. I was just trying to fix his hair." Vera slowly turned around toward the soldier.

Stephan's only recourse was to stay quiet as he tried to figure out what Vera was up to.

"Yes, I'll give you our passports. Can you tell me how long this is going to take? We need to get to Munich as soon as possible. This is a matter of life and death." Vera could hear her voice cracking.

Her mind was racing back and forth, back and forth. *Now is not the time to be frightened*, she told herself.

"A few years ago, my cousin here was in a terrible car accident and he suffered terrible injuries to his brain and his spine."

Vera could feel her palms and forehead becoming damp.

"Actually, the doctors called his case an incredible miracle. He wasn't expected to survive. They thought he would be dead by now. Unfortunately, he can hardly move. He gets excruciating headaches, the pain is unbearable."

Vera put her hand on Stephan's shoulder and squeezed it as hard as she could.

Suddenly Stephan started to scream. "Ahhhhhhhhhhh!"

"You see what I mean? I'm sorry but I get too emotional seeing him in such a pain. To make things even worse, a moving bicycle hit him a few days ago, and now I've got to take him to a specialist. He's pretty bad."

"Ahhhhhhhh! It hurts so badly." Stephan screamed again.

"It is imperative that he sees this specialist right away. Time is of the essence. We've come from Vienna. His doctor ordered me to take him to Munich before it is too late. We don't want any delay. His doctor told me to give you this." She slipped some money into the soldier's hand.

"I cannot accept this." He handed back the money.

"Why not? This is not from me—it is from a doctor who is asking your help to save a human being's life. I don't understand what you possibly want with my cousin."

"I believe that this is Lucas...Stephan Lucas."

"Lucas? What Lucas?" Vera pretended to be surprised. "His name is Hundertwasser...Josef Hundertwasser."

"We are watching for a young man who escaped from Prague and is wanted by the KGB for criminal activity. He is an anti-Communist trying to overthrow the government. His name is Stephan Lucas and he is charged with conspiracy, extortion, robbery, gun possession, and possibly murder. He is armed and considered very dangerous. He is also traveling with a blonde woman who fits your description."

I am not going to be able to pull this off...Don't fall apart now, Vera kept telling herself.

"Oh! Now I know where I have heard that name. In Vienna, I heard that the police arrested him today outside of Prague." Vera took a deep breath. "I heard it at the train station right before we boarded this train."

"Are you sure?"

Come on, take charge...stay in control, Vera told herself.

Nervously, she pressed on. "Well, people were talking about this Lucas person...He is an anarchist fighting against the government. He is wanted for some bomb explosion also and he might have killed someone...didn't he?"

"That's right…" The soldier hesitated.

"I heard they shot and killed the blonde woman who was with him." Vera looked right at his eyes.

"Really?"

"Anyway, I cannot be worried about this Lucas. I need to get to Munich as soon as possible. Here are our passports." Vera interrupted the guard as she handed him the passports to inspect.

"As you will see, I'm Maria Kokoschka and this is my cousin Josef Hundertwasser. My cousin can barely walk and might die soon if I don't get him to Munich." She paused for a second to get her composure back.

"Don't you think it would look very bad if people started talking about how you didn't let a dying man get to the hospital on time because he looked like some anarchist?"

"But…" the soldier started to say.

Vera interrupted him again. "I told you, my cousin can barely walk…how can you think he is running around setting off bombs and killing people?"

"I'm not saying that…"

Vera interrupted him again. "Do you want it on your conscious? If he dies your name will be all over the news. I can see it now…RUSSIAN SOLDIER SHOWS NO COMPASSION WHEN KILLING HANDICAPPED MAN."

Stephan's mind worked very quickly. He could sum up a situation and act almost instantly.

"Oh! My head!" Stephan cried, putting both his hands to his forehead. "My head! It seems as if it will burst! Ahhhhh...Where am I? Who are you? I can't see!"

The soldier looked at them.

"Excuse me." Vera pushed past the soldier and started caressing Stephan's forehead. "Be brave. We will soon be in Munich. Hold on a little longer."

Vera turned and looked at the soldier. "Don't you understand the situation? Can you please help me? You are breaking my heart and killing my poor cousin."

The soldier had raised his eyebrows trying to figure out if Vera was telling the truth. "Wait here." He walked toward the other two soldiers. They held a hurried consultation as they examined the passports.

Vera could feel them glaring in her direction so she turned and looked out the window, sensing their suspicion. She was afraid to look at them, fearing they might be able to see how frightened she really was.

She knew her luck and charm would not save them every time *Please, God, help us one more time. That's all I ask of you.*

After a few minutes, the soldier came back. Vera felt like she was going to faint.

The soldier looked at her and, after an officious gesture, he handed the passports back to her, saying, "I know that such a beautiful woman like you would not lie to me. You are free to stay on the train. I wish you all the luck with your cousin."

For a split second, the soldier looked at Vera's hands as they trembled when she took the passports from him.

"Thank you so much." Vera smiled and started turning toward Stephan.

The soldier studied her for a moment before saying, "Wait!"

Vera closed her eyes. She thought he had changed his mind.

"...In regard to the doctor's wishes..."

"Oh that! Of course, here it is." Vera smiled as she slipped the money back into his hand.

The soldiers exited the train car as the train engine started again.

XXXIII

As the train started to move, Vera collapsed back on her seat. She couldn't stop shaking. She turned and looked at Stephan as they smiled at each other. Both could feel their bodies start to relax. They were now on their way to Salzburg, traveling with their false passports.

Vera closed her eyes and Stephan continued staring at Vera.

"Darling, you were incredible! I'm so proud of you. You have no idea. You were remarkable. I'm totally surprised at how you pulled all that together. Today was your turn to save my life." Stephan's voice grew enthusiastic.

Vera opened her eyes, "I'm still in shock, and I cannot believe we were able to pull this off. Darling, give me a few minutes to compose myself." She was consumed with exhaustion.

They were staring out the window at the beautiful mountains and countryside. The sky was clear and it was a balmy spring evening. They still couldn't believe they had made it that far. Both of them were in a daze looking at the spectacular scenery.

"I'm afraid to move, it feels like a dream, and I don't want to wake up," Stephan whispered in Vera's ear.

Stephan took her hand and both sat silently.

When they arrived in Salzburg it was sunny day.

Stephan jumped from the train to the platform and started yelling, "We are free! Free!" He was so happy, nothing else mattered. Vera looked at him and smiled.

"Darling, you don't know how wonderful is to be able to move freely around town, no longer having to hide in fear." Stephan smiled.

"Yes, this is so wonderful!" Vera put her arms around him.

As he left the station, Vera wondered what hotel they should go to. She turned to Stephan and asked, "I suppose we ought to be look for a place to stay…eh?"

Stephan looked into her eyes and said softly, "Right now, I just want to embrace you and take a long walk in this beautiful city. We are free, remember? Let's go for a walk first and find a place to stay on our way back from our walk."

They walked around the narrow streets of Salzburg looking at the beautiful baroque architecture and the spacious squares.

Architecturally, Vera and Stephan agreed, Salzburg had to be one of the most beautiful cities in Europe.

The city is nestled beneath the cliffs of the Hochberg, a rocky hill that is topped by the massive fortress of the Hohensalzburg.

Stephan and Vera walked up the hill to find the most

spectacular view of the city. It felt like a beautiful dream. Baroque towers and many churches dominated the city's skyline. At the other end of Salzburg, they could see the reflection of the sun on the flowing blue glacier water of the Salzach River.

Stephan and Vera were holding hands, admiring the view. "Oh! By the way, did you know that Salzburg means castle of the salt? That is because their main economic source used to be rock salt. At one point salt was considered to be a very rare and precious commodity and was as valuable as gold," Stephan mentioned.

Vera smiled as she was looking up at the Alps. It was like a fairytale. Everything was perfect, and snow blanketed the mountaintops. Vera's silky blonde hair covered half of her face, while the sunlight shone on the other half.

"God! You look like an angel. You are so beautiful." Stephan put his arms around her and they started kissing passionately.

"We better find a place to stay. I want to make love to my angel," Stephan whispered into her ear.

They found a nice small hotel two blocks from the train station.

The following morning Vera and Stephan went and registered with the IRO, the International Refugee Organization.

"Now we are set to find living accommodations outside the refugee camp." Stephan hugged Vera. They felt very happy.

They went looking for a place to live and found a room in a private two-story house, a charming wooden dwelling with a sloping roof and wide overhanging eaves.

The house belonged to an older Czech couple named Tony and Amalie. Both of them had left Czechoslovakia before the Communist takeover.

Tony was a very quiet man of medium height with beautiful white hair.

Amalie was a stocky middle-aged woman with wavy brown hair. She was always elegantly dressed. The frame of her glasses needed tightening so she was constantly pushing them up in order to see. Her smile was warm and caring.

The couple's only child had been killed in a concentration camp. Amalie was taken aback by the fact that Stephan reminded her of her son. Right away, the couple treated Stephan like an adopted son.

Everything was falling into place.

Vera and Stephan spent most of their time together going hiking, sightseeing, and reading. They acted like inseparable teenagers. They would spend hours talking to each other, sharing their deepest feelings. They would laugh for hours.

A few weeks went by and one morning, when Vera was

walking back from the local bakery, a strange feeling suddenly came over her.

She stopped and looked around, feeling that something had made her stop. She realized she had just walked past the house where Mozart was born and raised. Mozart was part of the culture of Salzburg. His family was buried in a small church graveyard in the old town. Fans from all over the world came to Mozart's birthplace.

That feeling brought a sense of déjà vu and Vera started to think about Harold. She remembered when both of them walked around Prague looking at some of the places where Mozart had stayed. She wondered what was happening in his life. *Did he still think about her?* She realized that she missed him and that it had been a long time since she had received any news from him. All sorts of memories went through her mind.

Vera started feeling melancholic and got the urge to contact him. So she decided to write him a postcard. *Sending him a postcard of Mozart's birthplace is perfect,* Vera thought to herself.

Dear Harold:

I hope everything is well with you. There have been so many changes in my life. I have escaped from Czechoslovakia and I'm living under the IRO protection in Salzburg. This postcard is the house

on Getreidegasse no. 9, where Mozart was born.
Fans from all over the word come to see it. I hope the
Italy address is still valid to reach you. I miss my
parents and my little Babushka very much.

I hope to hear from you soon. The best way to get in
touch with me is through the IRO address in Salzburg.
They will forward my mail.

Love always,

Veruska

She finished writing the postcard, and all of a sudden her mind drifted as she started agonizing about her parents. She was gripped with remorse that she had abandoned her family and that she resented her father for controlling every aspect of her life.

Her mind filled with images of her last argument with her father two days before she left. He had reprimanded her for coming home twenty minutes past her curfew.

Vladimir had looked displeased as he checked his watch, "Veruska, you are running late tonight. Where have you been? Why are you always disobeying me lately?"

Vera could not keep still any longer. She felt that he didn't want her around the house, that he wanted her out of the way so he could continue dominating her mother who was an emotionally codependent wife.

"But, Father," Vera had screamed back at him, "why

do you always criticize me?"

She could feel the blood rushing to her face.

"Everything I do is never good enough for you. You always tell me what I'm doing is wrong. Don't I do anything right? I was late twenty minutes late, TWENTY lousy minutes. Please believe me, Father, when I tell you I am an obedient daughter."

Vladimir hit the wall with his hand to interrupt Vera. "That is enough from you. You are under my care and my authority and therefore you will obey my rules." His voice had been harsher than usual and his eyes had turned cold, like ice.

Once he started pacing back and forth, with both hands behind his back, Vera instinctively knew it was an indication she had pushed her father as far as she could before his fury would erupt.

Clearly, there was nothing else Vera could say except, "Father, I have behaved very badly and I'm truly sorry. Please don't be angry. I don't mean to be disrespectful."

"You don't have to apologize. I understand," Vladimir had answered taking a deep breath. His face had softened a bit.

"May I go to my room?" Vera had asked softly.

"Yes, my daughter, you may."

Vera had walked to her room and jumped on her bed. Tears rolled down her face. She knew that after the confrontation with her father there was nothing else she could say. She figured out that both of them needed time to heal.

That was when Vera had realized she could no longer live under her father's tyranny.

At the same time, downstairs, Vladimir realized that his daughter had become an independent and liberated woman and he was no longer going to be able to control her life.

What would have happened with my life if I had stayed in Czechoslovakia? Vera asked herself. *What if I had become a nun? Perhaps I made the wrong decision and I should have stayed with my parents.* She felt so guilty.

Suddenly, Vera was jolted back to reality when the baby of the woman walking by started to cry. Quickly she realized she was still standing on the square in front of Mozart's birthplace.

Two months elapsed.

As each day went by, their love for each other grew more and more intense.

They roamed around Salzburg enjoying the beautiful scenery. Everything was so magical, the snow-capped mountains, the lakes, and the green valleys.

As time went by Vera started feeling isolated. She had no contact with her family and no news from Harold. Vera felt her love for Stephan was blossoming. She wanted to make sure she was falling in love with him for the right reasons and not because she felt lonely. She was terrified of becoming just like her mother—totally dependent on him.

One afternoon as the clouds started to break apart and the first strands of sunshine came through the clouds, Stephan turned to Vera and said. "Hooray! It's going to be a gorgeous afternoon—let's go for a walk."

They walked to Salzburg Cathedral and the fountain in the Residenzplatz. Stephan had is arms around Vera.

"What's wrong? Why are you acting so nervous?" Vera asked.

"Oh nothing. I'm just looking for something," Stephan whispered.

"For what?"

"You'll see when I find it...don't be so curious." Stephan laughed.

They started walking toward the Salzach River. Stephan was constantly looking at his watch.

"Darling, you are making me nervous. What's wrong?" Vera had a puzzled look on her face.

Stephan grabbed her hand and started pulling her. "Come with me! Hurry! Let's run!"

Vera started to giggle. "Stephan, have you gone mad?"

"Come on, run, please hurry."

They ran for one minute until they reached the top of a

foothill. When they stopped, they were overlooking a most spectacular view. The sun was beginning to set behind the Festung Hohensalzburg Castle. There were just enough clouds in the sky to create a soft fading golden glow floating around the silhouette of the baroque towers and churches. To the left they could see an open area filled with colorful wildflowers. Behind the city, they could see the rising snow-capped mountains. The Alps formed a powerful backdrop for their picture-perfect view.

It was exactly six o'clock in the afternoon.

Stephan turned and looked into the eyes of the woman he loved. He slowly knelt in front of Vera and whispered, "You know how much I love you?" As he spoke, like magic all the church bells around them rang. "The bells in my heart will ring as loud as the church bells that you now hear if you would marry me...Veruska, will you marry me?"

Vera nodded as her eyes filled with tears. "Oh, my God! Yes, of course I will."

Vera started crying.

They embraced each other and kissed.

The first few months of their union were all about love. Life was a paradise. They played together like two kids with no worries.

Vera and Stephan spent the rest of that year in Salzburg. As the time passed, their love grew stronger.

One morning, Stephan walked their room and said,

"This was the longest year of our lives, we were not allowed to work because we are not Austrians."

Vera smiled and rolled her eyes agreeing with Stephan.

"Today is the day that everything will change because today is our one year anniversary in Salzburg. Darling, do you know what that means?"

"Yes,…but of course. We can finally move on."

"Yes, after one year we are now eligible to proceed to whichever country will grant us asylum. Right now there are two possibilities…either Australia or Canada."

Vera paused for a minute, contemplating her choices.

"I don't know too much about Australia and it seems so far away and…so isolated. My vote is to go to Canada."

"I just want to be with you so Canada here we come."

XXXIV

San Francisco, USA

The afternoon was warm; Harold was in his apartment, sitting in the leather sofa. The window was open and he was staring at the Golden State Bay Bridge.

It has been two months since he was transferred to the Brazilian Consulate in San Francisco.

Sipping a cafe au lait he looked at Vera's postcard which had taken six months to reach him from Salzburg.

Vera mailed it to his mother's address in Italy where it sat for four weeks while she was on vacation.

As Harold was in transition moving to Brazil, his mother waited another two months to forward the postcard to him. By the time it reached Brazil, he had already moved to San Francisco. Another few weeks went by until someone forward the postcard to him at the Brazilian Consulate in San Francisco.

He started writing a long letter to the woman he loved so deeply, hopping that it would reach its destination.

So many changes had happened to him. He had finally settled in San Francisco but felt guilty for leaving his mother back in Florence.

The move to San Francisco was necessary for him to continue pursing his dream of becoming a Brazilian diplomat.

He hadn't seen his father since the last time they had the big argument. As far as he was concerned his father didn't exist.

He closed his eyes and remembered when he had held Vera in his arms. He could still vividly feel her lips touching his, her silky hair brushing against his skin, the fire erupting inside him…a very strong burning desire.

Both their lives had become so complicated after he left Prague. He was so glad she was able to escape.

Will I ever see her again? Would our feelings still be the same? Where is she now? He asked himself.

XXXV

At the same time that Harold was writing her a letter, Stephan and Vera started their journey to Canada. Traveling by train they went through the Western Zone of Germany to Hamburg.

Once in Hamburg they were able to board a ship to Halifax, in Canada.

"Darling, can you believe we are on our way to a new life?" Vera asked.

"Here is to our new life." Stephan said giving Vera a big kiss.

From Halifax they took the train to Toronto where they contacted the representative of the International Refugee Organization.

The IRO had an agreement with the Canadian Government that in order for a displaced person to immigrate into Canada, they must serve one year indentured to a Canadian family willing to sponsor them. After that year, the Canadian Government would issue a "displaced person" document. With that official document they were allowed to go where they chose and to seek any type of employment.

The woman working for IRO explained to them that they could either be located in a big city such as Toronto or they could spend their first year in a rural area.

Stephan and Vera decided they would prefer a rural area.

"In this case, I have some good news," The woman said. "There is an opportunity for the two of you to spend your year together with a family who owns a peach orchard. Their farm is located just outside the city of Grimsby, not very far south of here."

"That's great!" Vera said, looking at Stephan.

The woman continued explaining, "They are a very nice family."

She turned and looked at Vera. "You will work as a house maid with the usual household duties. You will need to get up at six in the morning and start your daily chores. Your chores will include cleaning the toilets, scrubbing the bathroom and kitchen floors, dusting the furniture, cleaning the carpets, preparing meals and cleaning up afterwards."

"Do you have any questions?"

"No, this is great. I know I will adapt quickly to my duties." Vera smiled.

"Stephan," she turned to look at him. "You will work in the orchard, performing all the usual tasks required to maintain the farm. Your duties will include fertilizing the soil, picking peaches, packing them and transporting them to the market. There is a man named John who works in the orchard, he will explain and show you your duties."

The woman smiled at them. "Do you have any questions?"

"No questions, it sounds fine. Thank you very much."

said Stephan.

"One final point, you will live in your own room in the house, separate from the family."

The next morning, Stephan and Vera took the train to Grimsby. They were welcomed by the elderly couple, Fred and Mary Williams, owners of the farm. They were a very nice couple, grateful to have the help around the farm.

The year went by quickly and without incidents.

Stephan and Vera saved as much money as they could before they moved to Hamilton.

XXXVI

Stephan and Vera settled into a small apartment in Hamilton. Vera was employed as a teller in a bank while Stephan worked at night in an icehouse.

Wanting to improve their lifestyle, they looked for other ways to increase their income. Stephan started part time selling real estate while Vera worked extra hours in the bank.

Vera kept in constant communication with her parents through the mail. On average it would take three to four weeks for her letter to be delivered and they were never sure that all of them were delivered. They knew they had to be careful with the content of the letter as anyone working for the Communist government could open and read any letter.

Vera missed her parents and Babushka very much. She was glad that everything was going well with them except, of course, the living conditions in Czechoslovakia that did not improve. Corruption, shortage of food and necessities and lack of freedom were part of everyday living.

One night Vera came home from work, in dead winter, the cold weather was brutal.

As she walked in she started coughing uncontrollably.

"Darling, are you feeling alright?" Stephan asked. "You

don't look that well. And this continues cough."

"I'm fine, don't worry." Vera answered between her coughing attacks.

"I must be fighting a cold. I can feel it. I think I have a small fever."

"You don't look well. You look tired and it looks like you have lost some weight." Stephan had a worried look.

"Thanks! I love you too." Vera replied laughing.

She started coughing again. "Don't make me laugh because it makes me cough all the more."

"No, seriously. Have you not noticed that sometimes you have difficulty breathing?"

"If you are not better by tomorrow I'll take you to the doctor and no arguing with me."

In the middle of the night Vera got up, she was having chest pain and sweating. She started coughing so hard that she coughed up blood.

The next day she and Stephan went to the doctor.

"Well, we have to wait until we get the test results back. However, looking at the X-ray I have a good idea of what you have." Doctor Chumley told them..

"The good news is that what you have is treatable."

"Now, Doctor Chumley, you are scaring me if you are mention good news, then I assume there is also bad news." Vera tried to stay calm.

"What is the bad news, doctor?"

"The bad news is that it is going to take a long process to treat this."

"You are very lucky, we caught this in the early stages. You must start treatment right away so that it doesn't become a deadly disease."

Vera and Stephan stared at Doctor Chumley, scared and shocked.

"What you have is pulmonary tuberculosis; people refer to it as TB. Tuberculosis is one of the oldest diseases of humans. It is a contagious bacterial infection caused by *Mycobacterium tuberculosis*. The lungs are primarily involved, but the infection can spread to other organs."

He paused for a second.

"Until the 1800s, no treatment existed for tuberculosis. Families and their doctors could only helplessly watch a patient's downward path to death. Family members and friends frequently became infected and followed the same path to the grave. The bodies and property of those who died from tuberculosis were burned immediately." Doctor Chumley laughed. "But this is not the case now-a-days."

"How did Vera get TB?" Stephan asked. "This is hard to answer. Tuberculosis can develop after inhaling droplets sprayed into the air from coughing or sneezing by someone who has TB. The primary stage of the infection was probably contracted many years ago but for some reason or another it stayed in her system dormant without manifesting itself until now."

Vera started coughing again.

"The treatment for your TB is based on you spending time in a sanatorium. You are luck to be here in Canada. We are known for having the most updated treatment and we have enough sanatoriums to treat every case of TB."

"Sanatorium?" Vera mumbled.

"A Sanatorium is the place where you must stay for a cure."

"How many days will I have to stay there?" Vera asked.

"Well, it will be more then a few days, we are talking about months."

"Months?" Vera couldn't believe what she had heard.

Doctor Chumley sighed. "Probably close to one year."

"One year? Are you joking?" Vera felt very weak.

"I wish I was joking. Consider yourself luck. Until a few years ago the average stay at the sanatorium was about three to five years, sometimes longer."

Vera grabbed Stephan's hand and started to cough uncontrollably.

"Vera please try to relax"

"Relax?" Vera's voice became louder "My entire life is going to change and you want me to relax?"

Stephan turned and looked into Vera's eyes. "Darling,

please let's hear what else the doctor has to say. You know I would never forgive myself if something happened to you." Stephan smiled and squeezed her hand in support.

"You are right, please Doctor Chumley, continue."

"You will obviously have to give up your job and apply for the Government treatment program. The program will provide you with an allowance which will cover your board and room, clothing, and a $3.00 per month 'Comfort Allowance.' The 'Comfort Allowance' will pay for such items as stamps and haircuts."

"Once in the sanatorium you will see that the treatment is not that bad. It consists of lots of rest, fresh air, good nutrition and some sun. The sun helps kill TB bacteria. When the sun's UV rays reach the human skin, vitamin D is produced. This isolation is necessary to prevent the spread of the infection."

"This is much better then some of the old traditional treatments that included drinking potions of unsavory ingredients like garlic and dog fat, inhaling smoke from burning cow dung, and taking long sea voyages to exercise the chest with extended vomiting. French physicians once treated their patients by placing seaweed under their beds, noting that tuberculosis was less common among those living near the ocean."

Doctor Chumley smiled at Vera. "If you prefer we can use another old treatment such as you staying in an airtight room, wrapped in a feather blanket, near a hot stove."

"No thank you." Vera managed a laugh.

"If not that, here is another treatment that I can recommend. A long time ago doctors believed that TB was caused by evil spirits or odors from foul sewage or swamplands. The treatment included hypnosis, in addition to purging, blood-letting and other desperate measures."

"No thanks, again. I will stick with the traditional treatment used today."

"Good. Let's start making the arrangements so that you can immediately enter the Sanatorium."

That evening was Vera's first evening at the Sanatorium. She embraced Stephan tightly, afraid to let him go.

"Darling, you are going to break my bones. Everything will be fine. You will see. You will get used to this leisurely lifestyle and probably won't want to give it up. I wish I could join you."

Vera smiled.

The Sanatorium was located in the countryside just outside of the city. The gardens were very well kept and the nurses and attendants were very pleasant. Vera felt as she was living in a church, everything was very quiet and tranquil. There wasn't much to do, Vera spent most of her time resting, getting fresh air and a plentiful supply of nourishing food including milk and eggs which were considered essential.

She looked forward to Stephan's visits. She tried not asking him to come every day because of the long drive and once in the sanatorium there wasn't anything to do. Sometimes Vera would be totally exhausted from her illness and have a hard time staying awake while Stephan was there.

Although she usually felt tired, her heath seemed stable.

After a couple of months Stephan's visits started becoming less frequent.

Vera felt she was going crazy with boredom and wondered when Stephan would come to see her.

She spent hours sitting on a lounge-chair outside, wrapped in a blanket getting as much sun as possible. Having color on her face was the only way she felt healthy.

Another month went by and Stephan began calling with excuses why he could not come to see her.

"Hello darling. How are you feeling today? Would you mind if I don't come and see you? I really want to see you but I'm so exhausted from working so many hours."

Vera always tried not to sound too disappointed. "I miss you so much...Just stay home and get some rest."

Stephan claimed exhaustion, working late, not feeling well, flat tire, dinner with the boss. Vera wondered when he would run out of excuses.

The few time they did get together for any length of

time, they would always end up having a big fight.

"Why don't you want to talk about the future?...Our future?" Vera asked, as she started trembling showing her vulnerability.

"Look at the time. It is so late." Stephan looking at his watch.

"I must go. We will talk about it when you are stronger and healthier."

The months just started to come and go.

Stephan often grew impatient, even contemptuous toward Vera.

One rainy afternoon, Vera was staring at the water dripping outside from the tree branches. Stephan had called and told her he wasn't able to come and see her that afternoon because the roads were flooded from all the rain.

Vera could not help to feel signs of alienation and loneliness.

They were growing farther and farther apart. She felt that the warmth of feeling, the tenderness and the love that they once had, no longer existed.

She started to feel depression setting in as Stephan visits became more infrequent.

At the same time, Stephan's Casanova reputation resurfaced again.

It was rumored that Stephan had become quite a man about town as he had been seen in one of the topless clubs in town.

Vera was too proud to acknowledge that she had made a mistake in her choice of a husband.

She started to feel anxiety and nausea. Inside she wanted to cry.

Then one day, Vera really broke down and wept for a long time. She sank into deep depression, sobbing frequently, feeling very lonely. She felt the full power of remorse as she became melancholy; she feared the future.

Vera decided it was time for a change when she started suspecting that Stephan was having an affair.

She took hold of her thoughts and made her decision.

Vera waited until Stephan's next visit. She wore her white silk blouse tucked loosely into a pair of pleated pants, pulled up too high above her waist.

"Hello Stephan, I am glad you decided to show up today." Vera said as he walked into her room.

Don't you dare cry, you need to be strong. She told herself

"You are not going to start with this again." Stephan said irritably.

"Don't worry, I'm not starting anything. As a matter of fact, I'm going to make things easier for both of us." She looked straight at him.

Vera took a deep breath. "This is something I should have done months ago."

"Darling,..." Stephan started to say.

She raised her hand. "Let me finish! Please! Day after day you avoid coming here. In the last six months you have not even been tolerant of me." Vera stopped for a moment to see if Stephan would say anything.

"We have not been happy. Our marriage has proved to be a failure. Have you wondered what makes a marriage work?" Vera asked him.

"You cannot say that one particular factor is responsible for our marriage falling apart. It is a combination of many factors that have contributed to its failure." Stephan tried telling her.

"Well, it also doesn't help when you are having an affair does it?" Vera said sarcastically.

"Don't believe everything you hear."

"Stephan," she said, as her voice trembled a little, "for your sake and mine don't lie to me. Both of us know what the answer is." Vera bit her lip to keep silent, no use talking about the other woman.

It was an awkward silent.

"I also do not want us to continue pretending that everything is fine between us because in the end we would hate each other."

"I am now strong enough to face our fate!"

Vera looked up slowly at him.

"Our marriage is over." Vera spoke tenderly. "We will

be happier and better off leading our separate lives."

"I will always be thankful to you for risking your life to rescue me." She smiled.

"I also don't see any need to continue to talk about our failed marriage, so let's just say goodbye. Don't you agree?" Vera was trying to make her voice sound very casual.

"I would like us to think about our marriage and our commitment to each other before throwing it all away."

"Goodbye Stephan." Vera's female intuition kept telling her that it was all over.

Stephan made his way towards the door, he looked back at her. Her eyes were fixed in Stephan.

"Good bye Veruska, I'll be in touch."

After Stephan left the room Vera covered her face with her hands and sobbed for hours. She finally managed staggering to her bed where she continued crying.

Vera sat alone gazing into the darkness, she felt lost, and she felt terrified.

She curled into a ball and went to sleep.

The next morning Vera learned that Stephan had left her for another woman and that he wanted to marry her.

She knew she had to block it out of her mind. *Stephan didn't exist anymore.*

To make things worse, that same afternoon she received a telegram from Czechoslovakia. She seat on the edge of her bed. She could not believe what she was reading.

> *My darling daughter. Brace yourself for horrible news.*
> *Marek is dead. Cause of death unknown. Either*
> *drowned or shoot by guards. He was attempting to*
> *cross border to be with you. Please be careful.*
> *We love you very much.*
> *Vladimir.*

"Noooooooo! That cannot be true!" she screamed before collapsing on the floor.

Everything felt totally out of control. She wanted for everything to go away.

There was no reason to live.

She wanted to die.

XXXVII

"Well, here we are one year later and there are no more traces of TB, so you are free to go." Doctor Chumley and Vera were standing at the entrance of the sanatorium. Vera was waiting for a taxi to arrive to take her to the city so that she could find a place to live.

"What's next for you?" Doctor Chumley asked her.

"I'm not sure. I must find a place to stay and a job, basically I'm starting over." Vera smiled so he would not see how terrified she really was.

"Are you going to be alright?" The doctor was concerned about her.

"Oh yes. I have survived a Nazi occupation, a Communist takeover, escaping from the Communist by swimming across the Danube River and I have traveled under extremely dangerous circumstances."

Vera paused for a moment. "Oh! And as of today, I can add that I have survived TB and one year in a sanatorium." She giggled. "I definitely will survive a divorce."

"I must admit, I am concerned about you."

"You are very kind. I'll be fine. Two weeks ago I received a letter from the IRO organization telling me that a dear friend, Harold Coimbra was trying to contact me. As you may know, it is against the IRO regulations to reveal the whereabouts of any refugee. Instead they provided me with his address so that I can write to him should I desire. Presently he is in Brazil." Vera looked at the doctor and started laughing.

"I'm so sorry, here I'm taking about someone you don't even know. He was my first love. Who knows what might happen."

Doctor Chumley laughed before giving Vera a hug.

"I wish you all the luck in your new life."

"Thank you for everything." Vera told him before walking toward the approaching taxi.

Vera found a small one bedroom apartment, only three blocks away from the bank where she was able to get her job. The first thing she did after moving into her apartment was to write to Harold. A few weeks later she received his reply. They started writing to each other almost every day.

They acted as if nothing had happened during these last years.

A few months went by and one day a letter came from Harold asking her to come and see him in Brazil.

Vera danced around her apartment, elated, she could think only of him. She decided to take the first flight available to Rio de Janeiro.

Will we still have the same feelings for each other?

Will we still feel that incredible desire for each other? Are we still in love? She kept asking herself.

Two days later, Vera arrived at the Galeão International Airport.

The temperature was over 100 degrees and the humidity was close to 100 percent. Vera never experienced such heat or humidity. She felt like she was going to faint and wasn't sure if it was just nerves or the extreme heat.

She was glad she was wearing a nice black and tan cotton dress, black satin pumps with back ruffle trim and cat eye sunglasses. She had on a pale red lipstick and a touch of mascara.

Vera was one of the first passengers to go thought immigration and customs. When she came out into the waiting room there were hundreds of people waiting for passengers. As she looked around the crowd she could not see Harold.

As she looked at her watch, a voice behind her said, "Excuse me, I'm looking for Vera Pisova."

Recognizing his voice, she turned around and saw his bedroom eyes and beautiful smile. He was wearing a plaid coat, dark slacks, red tie and his round glasses and his face was tan from the sun. He was holding two dozen red roses. Momentarily they stared at each other.

That was the moment that both of them had been

dreaming off.

Vera looked beautiful, radiant and happy. Her eyes were sparkling. She dove into his arms.

"My God, you look more amazing than I ever remembered." Harold said before giving her a long kiss.

After a long hug and more kisses, Harold asked, "How did you manage to go through customs so fast?" At the same time he looked around the floor, "Where is your luggage?"

"No luggage. When I escape from Czechoslovakia I had to leave everything behind. Coming to Brazil represents another new beginning so I decided to leave everything behind again."

Harold laughed. "You are so crazy and so wonderful and so beautiful."

Again they kissed passionately. Both of them could feel a sexual desired starting to burn and take over their bodies. Harold wasn't sure how long he would be able to control himself. He had fantasized for so long about this day.

"Well let's go then." He said smiling.

As they exited the terminal there was a chauffer waiting for them.

"I hired a chauffer just for today. I want to spend every second of today next to you and looking at you. I am afraid that this might be a dream. Even if it is, do you realized I have dreamed about this moment for so long?"

He drew Vera closer to him.

She stood glaring at him as his face became full of passion and desire.

"Let's stop at a small boutique in Ipanema so you can buy some clothes."

After shopping at the boutique they drove to Harold's aunt house on the outskirts of Rio. It was a two story colonial plantation mansion on a small cliff overlooking the beach and the ocean. The house had eight bedrooms and nine bathrooms. The living room was a very spacious with an eclectic combination of modern and antique colonial furniture.

On one wall there were four sliding doors that opened onto a huge patio with a garden and a beautiful pool.

The view from the patio was breathtaking. The white sands of the beach were contrasted against the five different shades of blue of the ocean water, all the colors blending perfectly together.

A small rain forest surrounded the left side of the pool and extended all the way underneath the patio down to the beach. Large beautiful palm trees separated the rain forest from the fine white sands of the beach.

The overflow from the pool formed a waterfall that dropped below the patio near the rain forest and then down the cliff.

The waterfall felt in front of the exterior glass wall of

the master bedroom on the ground floor.

"Harold this is such a magnificent view, I have never seen anything like it. Everything is so exotic." Vera smiled seductively.

Harold looked at her very flirtatiously and said. "You are the one who is exotic. I will have to take you on a private exotic experience on that white sandy beach," he whispered in her ear, "preferably at night so it is more exotic."

"At what time, does the sun set in Rio de Janeiro?" Vera asked.

Both started too laughed.

They could feel the sexual tension mounting, just like when they where in Prague.

That evening the sky was clear and there was a nice warm breeze which made it a perfect evening to dine outside on the patio.

Harold was running around making sure everything was going to be perfect for their first evening together.

Vera took a long bath and when she walked onto the patio the sun had already set. Harold was lighting candles on the table which was set up with a beautiful flower arrangement of some of the most exotic Brazilian flowers.

"Everything looks so lovely." Vera was memorized by all of it. The experience of the last few years made her appreciate the small things in life.

Harold was wearing a lightweight casual shirt and a navy blue pants as was the custom in the heat of Rio. His black hair was gelled back and he was very tan.

"Do you realize how your tan face accentuates your beautiful green eyes?" Vera asked him.

Harold had stopped for a moment, memorized by Vera's beauty.

"No, I get tired of looking at myself, I would rather look at you instead. I still cannot believe that you are here."

Vera smiled at him. She was wearing a very elegant and sexy straight fitted dress with a Grecian twist, one of the purchases at the boutique. Her blond hair was down and curled at the ends. Her entire body moved sensually as she walked towards the dining table.

Harold kissed her and caressed her face. The caressing of his fingers, unleashed a strong desire within her. Both felt the heat of this desire pulling their bodies together.

While Harold went to put on some bossa nova music, Vera seated herself admiring the magnificent view of the white sandy beach, the dark ocean and the stars above her. She could hear the waves crashing down on the beach. There was a nice warm breeze was blowing. It was a perfect night.

When Harold returned he had brought two lime-soaked drinks.

"This is our traditional Brazilian drink called caipirinha. It is prepared with cachaça. Cachaça is distilled from sugar cane and it is probably the strongest drink you have ever taste. You crush the lime and add lots of sugar and then you pour the cachaça. The lime and the sugar will hide the taste of the cachaça."

"You are not trying to take advantage of me again, are you?" Vera laughed.

"No way! I am the one that have to be careful with you. You probably will take advantage of me."

They laughed.

Harold raised his glass and said, "I want to make a toast. Here is to the most beautiful woman I know. You don't know how many times I have dreamt about tonight."

"Hummm. This is so delicious." Vera smiled at Harold.

"Do you remember when we went to our first dinner together before the party and you made me try that famous Czech dumpling?"

"You mean Knedliky?"

"Correct! Well now it is going to be your turn to try our Brazilian dumplings. We are starting with coxinhas. Coxinha is a typical Brazilian entrée. It is a fried dumpling filled with a chicken paste. I hope you like it. After that we are having fillet mignon steak with rice and black beans, all prepared the Brazilian way."

After dinner Vera was sipping champagne and gazing at the stars. She was so happy, she wanted that moment to never end.

They had so much to talk about.

Harold was inside, supposedly tending to the dessert. A few minutes later he reappeared slightly out of breath.

Vera looked at him, wondering what he was up to.

"Dinner turned up well, didn't it?"

"Everything was delicious and delightful." Vera's voice was pleasing.

Harold smiled and looked at his watch.

"What is it? Why are you looking at the time?" He hesitated and smiled.

"Isn't it almost eleven o'clock?" Harold asked her doubtfully.

Vera looked at her watch and said. "Yes, three more minute. Why?"

From the corner of her eyes she could see three women walking toward them. They were part of a small all girls band and were playing some of the music that had been played at the party in the castle in Prague.

"Hummm Harold just what are you up to? Vera asked.

He grinned. "Nothing I just wanted to bring back some memories from our first date."

"Somehow I don't believe you," Vera was enthralled.

Harold reached for Vera's hand and pulled her up towards him. He kissed her quickly and turned her in the direction of the beach and the ocean.

"Harold, what's going on?" Vera continued laughing.

"Please just stand here, looking in this direction while, I go get more champagne."

"This is paradise. It is so beautiful and peaceful...."

All of a sudden, the most spectacular and intricate firework display started on the beach beneath them.

Harold stood behind her, embracing her. It was the most magnificent firework show Vera had ever seen. When the firework show stopped Vera turned around to kiss Harold but he said, "It's not over yet, just keep looking down the beach."

"More?" Vera sounded surprised.

He nodded.

The smoke from the fireworks slowly cleared as Vera continued to gaze at the beach.

At first glance, she thought there were lights on the sand.

"Now that the smoke is clearing I can see some light... it looks like there are candles on the beach." Vera squinted trying to see what was under all the smoke.

"Keep looking my darling." Harold was still standing behind her, holding her very closely.

"Yes, I was right, there are candle on the beach. This is so beautiful." Vera smiled.

"Keep looking." Harold was still holding her tightly.

Vera frowned. "Humm I can now see that the candles

are lined up in a perfect line. Are they pointing in this direction?"

"No, keep looking."

"Oh wait! The candles are lined up to create a picture....hmmm...isn't that right?"

Harold was quiet, holding her so she wouldn't move. Vera was very curious trying to figure out what the picture depicted.

"Oh wait! I get it! They are forming letters ....Veruska ! That is so beautiful you have my name in writing on the beach."

Harold smiled and again pointed towards the sand.

"Ah! There is more? Lets see Veruska will..."

Suddenly her lips began trembling and her eyes filled with tears.

"Veruska will you... marry me?" She repeated.

Vera turned and looked at him before repeating what the saw on the beach, "Veruska will you marry me?"

She swallowed and for a few seconds she was unable to say anything.

Harold took hold of her hand and knelt in front of her before saying.

"Veruska....

Veruska you are my angel.

You are my love.

You are the only woman I have ever loved.

You are the only woman I love.

You are the only woman I will always love.

You are the only woman that will make me happy.

Veruska will you marry me?

Veruska please say YES."

Harold reached inside his pocket, took out and opened a jewelry box. Inside was a beautiful diamond engagement ring with silver setting.

"Veruska, I felt in love with you from the first moment I saw you. I have always loved you and I always will love you." His voice was warm and full of love.

Vera stood still for awhile, consumed by emotions.

Finally she was able to speak.

Tears rolled down her face.

"Darling, I...I need to tell you something before I can give you an answer."

XXXVIII

Harold was standing next to Vera waiting for her to continue.

"I...I don't want to hide anything from you therefore I feel the need to tell this..."

"Go on Darling!, I am listening."

"My other ..." Vera paused, wondering how to tell him, "my other marriage."

"You marriage with Stephan...right? Harold asked, puzzled. "I received your letter telling me everything"

"No, his name was..." she avoided his eyes, "after... after you left Czechoslovakia, my father decided he was the only person that could make a logical choice to find the right spouse for his little girl. He didn't want to run the risk of me choosing the wrong man."

"What??" Harold raised his voice.

"Please let me explain..."

Vera looked away and closed her eyes as she started to remember her conversation with Vladimir.

"But, Father! I am in love with Harold and we are..." Vera was unable to keep quiet.

"Nonsense! Don't interrupt me, my daughter, let me

finish." Vladimir raised his voice.

"Harold is not coming back. He was a very charming young man but if he is like his father who has a manicurist as a mistress I guarantee you that he already has a new Italian girlfriend."

"No! NO! He promised…"

Vladimir snapped at Veruska as he was not ready to be interrupted.

"For Christ sake you are going to believe someone that you only known for ten days? Don't be so naïve. You are eighteen years old and if you don't get married soon you will become an old maid…"

Vera couldn't look at Vladimir as she kept wondering if the real reason for his decision was the fact that he started to resented her because she started influencing her mother to be more independent

"One of the benefit of being a doctor is to have access to the right information to pick the right spouse for you. Someone with similar religious, political and cultural background…" Vladimir said. "I already found the perfect candidate for you; his name is Pavel Havel…he is an accountant for Barradov Studios so I valued him as an excellent spouse material and he has no preexisting medical conditions…"

"Go on." Said Harold.

"Darling, without you I felt so alone...I had nowhere to turn. I wasn't attracted to Pavel but I decided to take a chance because I could no longer live under my father's rules So I did my best to act as everything was perfect."

Vera paused before taking a depth breath.

"Two months after my first date with Pavel, my father decided it was time for us to get married. My parents planned and paid for the ceremony that was held at the Valdštejnský Palace."

Vera managed to smile.

"My father was convinced that he picked the right spouse for me so if was up to me to make my marriage work. His only advice to me was to always obey and respect my husband.."

Harold was silent.

"Two days after my wedding I started wondering, "What now?"

Vera turned around and tried looking at Harold.

"That was when I realized that Pavel and I had nothing in common. There was no chemistry between us. Two months later Pavel confessed that he was having an affair with an actress named Natasha Badactrissky."

Vera just wanted for Harold to put his arms around her.

"As you can imagine my father was furious when he found out. I moved back to my parents' house. Vladimir took all the wedding pictures and burned them. My marriage was annulled and we never talked about his bad decision again."

Harold and Vera stood next to each other looking at the ocean.

Vera started crying helplessly as she didn't know what else to say.

"Well this certainly change everything."

"What do you mean??"

"Remember what you told me when we were at the train station?...you said 'I love you, my darling! I will wait for you!' Now I am finding out that your idea of waiting for me is to be married twice."

Vera didn't know what to say.

"Now I know what we need to do..."

Harold had turned around and was staring at Vera.

"We cannot get married..."

Vera took a step backward. She could not believe what she was hearing.

Her heart was breaking apart.

There was a long and unbearable silence between them.

What am I supposed to do now? I have nothing and nowhere to go...

Suddenly her thoughts were interrupted when she heard Harold voice again, "We cannot get married until you promise me that you will do exactly what your father told you to do...'to always obey me and do what I tell you to do because you are my woman and you belong to me!"

Harold started to laugh.

Vera turned around and said, "That was cruel...I cannot believe you made me think ..."

They started laughing again.

"That wasn't funny." Vera slapped Harold's head.

Harold grabbed her and kissed her before saying, "Don't be mad. Don't you realize how much I love you? I'm the luckiest guy in the world....You still need to answer my question...*Veruska will you marry me?*"

Vera stared into Harold's eyes. "I should say NO!"

Vera started to laugh.

"Yes! Yes my darling! I will marry you! I love you!"

Tears rolled down her face.

"I love you." Harold said again before he kissed her passionately,

Harold took her hand and led her toward the beach to look at the burning candles.

The beach was deserted. Vera took off her shoes and began running and jumping around and over the candles. This was the happiest moment of her life. She acted like a little girl.

"Do you realize that you have changed my life? You are the most wonderful man I have ever met. You have made my life perfect."

Harold listened to her as he admired her flawless beautiful complexion.

Vera had a seductive style of her own and a very natural magnetic charm.

She knew he wanted her as much as she wanted him. She was gripped by passion.

Vera walked towards the ocean, stood at the edge of the beach letting the waves wet her feet. She looked up at the stars while enjoying the warm breeze blowing on her face and all over her body. The warm breeze made her feel very much alive and very sensual.

She turned around Harold walked towards her, she stared right into his eyes. He put his arms around her and lifted her up into the air before he gently laid her down on the soft white sand. His body was right next to hers.

Vera tossed back her blond hair

His strong arms held her in a long, tight embrace as he slowly started kissing her and undressing her. He was feeling her warm flesh and her nakedness. The caressing of his fingers unleashed an incredible desire to touch and explore every inch of her body.

Feeling the heat coming from his naked body and her desire for him .they rolled around the sand. Their bodies were rubbing against each other. Sweat was dripping from their bodies.

All of a sudden, a nice refreshing wave splashed all over their bodies.

Vera gasped and let out soft moan of pleasure.

They could taste their salty skins. Vera looked very seductively at him.

He couldn't stop looking at her.

They were being consumed by passion and desire for each other.

Their bodies were locked together as one.

They couldn't stop.

Their bodies were now moving in the same synchronized direction as they made passionate love.

XXXIX

The following morning, Vera decided there was no reason to go back to Canada; she just needed a divorce from Stephan.

Unfortunately, she could not get divorced in Brazil because at that time divorce was not legalized in Brazil.

One day later Harold returned to the house where they were staying and told Vera, "I have just been in a meeting with a lawyer and because divorce is not legalized in Brazil, our only solution is to start divorce proceedings in Uruguay where divorce is legal. It will take a little longer but it will solve the problem. "

"Well, that will give you more time to change your mind." Vera giggled.

"Don't be silly. Don't you know how much I love you?" Harold smiled at her.

"No as much as I love you." She said, looking straight into his eyes.

While waiting for Vera's divorce to be finalized, Harold and Vera moved to San Francisco so Harold could resume his diplomatic duties.

Seven months later Vera's divorce was finalized.

Meanwhile, Vera and Harold's love for each other grew deeper and deeper.

Right after Vera's divorced was finalized, Harold ran into another stumbling block.

"What's wrong, darling?" Vera asked Harold. She could sense there was something on his mind.

"Sit down, we need to talk." His face was very serious.

Vera's heart stared pounding very fast as she sensed something was terrible wrong.

"I just found out one more thing we will have to make a decision on."

"What is it?" Vera managed a smile.

"Well, there is regulation in the Brazilian Diplomatic Corps that anyone working for the Diplomatic Corps cannot take as a spouse someone who escaped from a Communist country."

"What? So you cannot marry me? This certain complicates things doesn't?" Vera looked away from him.

"That's right, our diplomats cannot marry anyone who escaped from Communism because it could jeopardize Brazil's relations with any communist countries. Actually, it goes farther than that, even if we were able to convince them that somehow you managed to leave Czechoslovakia if I marry a non-Brazilian woman it would preclude my advancement in the diplomatic corps."

Veruska's heart was breaking apart.

There was a long and unbearable silence between them. Vera was trying to think though all the implications of what Harold had told her. She could feel her stomach turning.

"Well there is only one solution." Vera said as she looked away from Harold. She knew if she looked at him she would break down and cry.

Harold was puzzled. "Hummm?"

"The only solution is for you to pursue your career and we'll not marry. Things might change some day but you cannot give up your dream because of me."

After hours of agonizing discussions on what to do, Harold took a break and went out for a short walk.

When he returned he sat next to Vera and grabbed her hand. Without hesitation, Harold said "You are right, this is a decision I must make so I don't regret it later."

Harold took a deep breath, before he continued. "Becoming an ambassador is my biggest dream, a dream I have had since I was a small kid so I would be totally crazy to give it up now. You know I would probably regret it later."

Vera looked down at the floor.

There was a brief silence before she started saying, "Hmmm I...I understand."

"Shhhhh! Let me finish, please!" Harold put his fingers on her lips, "Yes, it would be crazy for me to give up this dream. However, it would be even crazier to give up the biggest dream of my life. That would be letting go of the woman I love. Becoming an ambassador would mean nothing to me if I cannot share it with the woman I love. You are part of me and I want to spend the rest of my life with you."

Vera had mixed feelings; she looked up. "But…"

"No buts! Remember when we were at the train station in Prague and I promised that someday we would be together again? Well, now is the time for us to be together again so I'm asking you… Veruska will you marry me?"

She remembered what Babushka had once told her; *don't ever stand in the way of real love. Love is everything.*

"I, uh, well, I don't know… your career, your dream, you cannot…"

Harold placed his fingers over her lips again.

"Veruska will you marry me? We will have to move back to Brazil. I cannot guarantee what type of job I will find." He looked at her angelic face.

"If you don't want to marry me because you don't know what our financial situation will be, I totally understand and I don't blame you for…"

"Now it is your turn to be quiet …" Her eyes were filled with tears. "Yes, Yes my darling! My answer is Yes, I will marry you. I love you so much."

Vera had decided to follow her heart. Vera told herself

Don't you be a fool! For once in your life, just accept the fact that Harold choose you. He loves you and all he wants is for us to be together. Don't you be crazy and let go of love."

Vera hugged and kissed him passionately.

Deep inside she knew that she was making the right decision.

Four months later Veruska and Harold were married. Harold resigned from the embassy and they were on their way to Brazil.

Veruska

Veruska

www.ingramcontent.com/pod-product-compliance
Lightning Source LLC
Chambersburg PA
CBHW052024020726
47501CB00004B/1224